Great Stories for Children

Ruskin Bond has been writing for over sixty years, and has now over 120 titles in print—novels, collection of short stories, poetry, essays, anthologies and books for children. His first novel, *The Room on the Roof*, received the prestigious John Llewellyn Rhys Award in 1957. He has also received the Padma Shri (1999), the Padma Bhushan (2014) and two awards from Sahitya Akademi—one for his short stories and another for his writings for children. In 2012, the Delhi government gave him its Lifetime Achievement Award.

Born in 1934, Ruskin Bond grew up in Jamnagar, Shimla, New Delhi and Dehradun. Apart from three years in UK, he has spent all his life in India, and now lives in Mussoorie with his adopted family.

Dearest Archit,

Loads of love from Mansi

Swati

6th February 2022

By the Same Author

Angry River
A Little Night Music
A Long Walk for Bina
Hanuman to the Rescue
Ghost Stories from the Raj
Strange Men, Strange Places
The India I Love
Tales and Legends from India
The Blue Umbrella
Ruskin Bond's Children's Omnibus
Romi and the Wildfire
When the Tiger was King
School Days
School Times
Funny Side Up
Roads to Mussoorie
All Roads Lead to Ganga
The Rupa Book of Great Animal Stories
The Rupa Book of True Tales of Mystery and Adventure
The Rupa Book of Ruskin Bond's Himalayan Tales
The Rupa Book of Great Suspense Stories
The Rupa Laughter Omnibus
The Rupa Book of Haunted Houses
The Rupa Book of Travellers' Tales
The Rupa Book of Great Crime Stories
The Rupa Book of Nightmare Tales
The Rupa Book of Shikar Stories
The Rupa Book of Love Stories
The Rupa Book of Wicked Stories
The Rupa Book of Heartwarming Stories
The Rupa Book of Thrills and Spills
The Rupa Carnival of Terror
The Rupa Book of Snappy Surprises
Shudders in the Dark
Stories Short and Sweet

Great Stories for Children

Ruskin Bond

RUPA

Published by
Rupa Publications India Pvt. Ltd 2011
7/16, Ansari Road, Daryaganj
New Delhi 110002

Sales centres:
Allahabad Bengaluru Chennai
Hyderabad Jaipur Kathmandu
Kolkata Mumbai

This is a work of fiction. Names, characters, places and incidents are either the product of the author's imagination or are used fictitiously and any resemblance to any actual person, living or dead, events or locales is entirely coincidental.

ISBN: 978-81-291-1892-9

Thirty-fifth impression 2021

40 39 38 37 36 35

Printed at Rakmo Press Pvt. Ltd, New Delhi

Contents

A Special Tree

One day, when Rakesh was six, he walked home from the Mussoorie bazaar eating cherries. They were a little sweet, a little sour; small, bright red cherries, which had come all the way from the Kashmir Valley.

Here in the Himalayan foothills where Rakesh lived, there were not many fruit trees. The soil was stony, and the dry cold winds stunted the growth of most plants. But on the more sheltered slopes there were forests of oak and deodar.

Rakesh lived with his grandfather on the outskirts of Mussoorie, just where the forest began. His father and mother lived in a small village fifty miles away, where they grew maize and rice and barley in narrow terraced fields on the lower slopes of the mountain. But there were no schools in the village, and Rakesh's parents were keen that he should go to school. As soon as he was of school-going age, they sent him to stay with his grandfather in Mussoorie.

He had a little cottage outside the town.

Rakesh was on his way home from school when he bought the cherries. He paid fifty paise for the bunch. It took him about half-an-hour to walk home, and by the time he reached the cottage there were only three cherries left.

'Have a cherry, Grandfather,' he said, as soon as he saw his grandfather in the garden.

Grandfather took one cherry and Rakesh promptly ate the other two. He kept the last seed in his mouth for some time, rolling it round and round on his tongue until all the tang had gone. Then he placed the seed on the palm of his hand and studied it.

'Are cherry seeds lucky?' asked Rakesh.

'Of course.'

'Then I'll keep it.'

'Nothing is lucky if you put it away. If you want luck, you must put it to some use.'

'What can I do with a seed?'

'Plant it.'

So Rakesh found a small space and began to dig up a flowerbed.

'Hey, not there,' said Grandfather, 'I've sown mustard in that bed. Plant it in that shady corner, where it won't be disturbed.'

Rakesh went to a corner of the garden where the earth was soft and yielding. He did not have to dig. He pressed the seed into the soil with his thumb and it went right in.

Then he had his lunch, and ran off to play cricket with his friends, and forgot all about the cherry seed.

When it was winter in the hills, a cold wind blew down from the snows and went *whoo-whoo-whoo* in the deodar trees, and the garden was dry and bare. In the evenings Grandfather and Rakesh sat over a charcoal fire, and Grandfather told Rakesh stories – stories about people who turned into animals, and ghosts who lived in trees, and beans that jumped and stones that wept – and in turn Rakesh would read to him from the newspaper, Grandfather's eyesight being rather weak. Rakesh found the newspaper very dull – especially after the stories – but Grandfather wanted all the news...

They knew it was spring when the wild duck flew north again, to Siberia. Early in the morning, when he got up to chop wood and light a fire, Rakesh saw the V–shaped formation streaming northward, the calls of the birds carrying clearly through the thin mountain air.

One morning in the garden he bent to pick up what he thought was a small twig and found to his surprise that it was well rooted. He stared at it for a moment, then ran to fetch Grandfather, calling, 'Dada, come and look, the cherry tree has come up!'

'What cherry tree?' asked Grandfather, who had forgotten about it. 'The seed we planted last year – look, it's come up!'

Rakesh went down on his haunches, while Grandfather bent almost double and peered down at the tiny tree. It was about four inches high.

'Yes, it's a cherry tree,' said Grandfather. 'You should water it now and then.'

Rakesh ran indoors and came back with a bucket of water.

'Don't drown it!' said Grandfather.

Rakesh gave it a sprinkling and circled it with pebbles.

'What are the pebbles for?' asked Grandfather.

'For privacy,' said Rakesh.

He looked at the tree every morning but it did not seem to be growing very fast, so he stopped looking at it except quickly, out of the corner of his eye. And, after a week or two, when he allowed himself to look at it properly, he found that it had grown – at least an inch!

That year the monsoon rains came early and Rakesh plodded to and from school in raincoat and chappals. Ferns sprang from the trunks of trees, strange-looking lilies came up in the long grass, and even when it wasn't raining the trees dripped and mist came curling up the valley. The cherry tree grew quickly in this season.

It was about two feet high when a goat entered the garden and ate all the leaves. Only the main stem and two thin branches remained.

'Never mind,' said Grandfather, seeing that Rakesh was upset. 'It will grow again, cherry trees are tough.'

Towards the end of the rainy season new leaves appeared on the tree. Then a woman cutting grass scrambled down the hillside, her scythe swishing through the heavy monsoon foliage. She did not try to avoid the tree: one sweep, and the cherry tree was cut in two.

When Grandfather saw what had happened, he went after the woman and scolded her; but the damage could not be repaired.

'Maybe it will die now,' said Rakesh.

'Maybe,' said Grandfather.

But the cherry tree had no intention of dying.

By the time summer came round again, it had sent out several new shoots with tender green leaves. Rakesh had grown taller too. He was eight now, a sturdy boy with curly black hair and deep black eyes. 'Blackberry eyes,' Grandfather called them.

That monsoon Rakesh went home to his village, to help his father and mother with the planting and ploughing and sowing. He was thinner but stronger when he came back to Grandfather's house at the end of the rains to find that the cherry tree had grown another foot. It was now up to his chest.

Even when there was rain, Rakesh would sometimes water the tree. He wanted it to know that he was there.

One day he found a bright green praying-mantis perched on a branch, peering at him with bulging eyes. Rakesh let it remain there; it was the cherry tree's first visitor.

The next visitor was a hairy caterpillar, who started making a meal of the leaves. Rakesh removed it quickly and dropped it on a heap of dry leaves.

'Come back when you're a butterfly,' he said.

Winter came early. The cherry tree bent low with the weight of snow. Field-mice sought shelter in the roof of the cottage. The road from the valley was blocked, and for several days there was no newspaper, and this made Grandfather quite grumpy. His stories began to have unhappy endings.

In February it was Rakesh's birthday. He was nine – and the tree was four, but almost as tall as Rakesh.

One morning, when the sun came out, Grandfather came into the garden to 'let some warmth get into my bones,' as he put it. He stopped in front of the cherry tree, stared at it for a few moments, and then called out, 'Rakesh! Come and look! Come quickly before it falls!'

Rakesh and Grandfather gazed at the tree as though it had performed a miracle. There was a pale pink blossom at the end of a branch.

The following year there were more blossoms. And suddenly the tree was taller than Rakesh, even though it was less than half his age. And then it was taller than Grandfather, who was older than some of the oak trees.

But Rakesh had grown too. He could run and jump and climb trees as well as most boys, and he read a lot of books, although he still liked listening to Grandfather's tales.

In the cherry tree, bees came to feed on the nectar in the blossoms, and tiny birds pecked at the blossoms and broke them off. But the tree kept blossoming right through the spring, and there were always more blossoms than birds.

That summer there were small cherries on the tree. Rakesh tasted one and spat it out.

'It's too sour,' he said.

'They'll be better next year,' said Grandfather.

But the birds liked them – especially the bigger birds, such as the bulbuls and scarlet minivets – and they flitted in and out of the foliage, feasting on the cherries.

On a warm sunny afternoon, when even the bees looked sleepy, Rakesh was looking for Grandfather without finding him in any of his favourite places around the house. Then he looked out of the bedroom window and saw Grandfather reclining on a cane chair under the cherry tree.

'There's just the right amount of shade here,' said Grandfather. 'And I like looking at the leaves.'

'They're pretty leaves,' said Rakesh. 'And they are always ready to dance, if there's a breeze.'

After Grandfather had come indoors, Rakesh went into the garden and lay down on the grass beneath the tree. He gazed up through the leaves at the great blue sky; and turning on his side, he could see the mountains striding away into the clouds. He was still lying beneath the tree when the evening shadows crept across the garden. Grandfather came back and sat down beside Rakesh, and they waited in silence until the stars came out and the nightjar began to call. In the forest below, the crickets and cicadas began tuning up; and suddenly the trees were full of the sound of insects.

'There are so many trees in the forest,' said Rakesh. 'What's so special about this tree? Why do we like it so much?'

'We planted it ourselves,' said Grandfather. That's why it's special.'

'Just one small seed,' said Rakesh, and he touched he smooth bark of the tree that he had grown. He an his hand along the trunk of the tree and put his inger to the tip of a leaf. 'I wonder,' he whispered. Is this what it feels to be God?'

The School Among the Pines

1

A leopard, lithe and sinewy, drank at the mountain stream, and then lay down on the grass to bask in the late February sunshine. Its tail twitched occasionally and the animal appeared to be sleeping. At the sound of distant voices it raised its head to listen, then stood up and leapt lightly over the boulders in the stream, disappearing among the trees on the opposite bank.

A minute or two later, three children came walking down the forest path. They were a girl and two boys, and they were singing in their local dialect an old song they had learnt from their grandparents.

Five more miles to go!
We climb through rain and snow.
A river to cross...
A mountain to pass...
Now we've four more miles to go!

Their school satchels looked new, their clothes had been washed and pressed. Their loud and cheerful singing startled a Spotted Forktail. The bird left its favourite rock in the stream and flew down the dark ravine.

'Well, we have only three more miles to go,' said the bigger boy, Prakash, who had been this way hundreds of times. 'But first we have to cross the stream.'

He was a sturdy twelve-year-old with eyes like raspberries and a mop of bushy hair that refused to settle down on his head. The girl and her small brother were taking this path for the first time.

'I'm feeling tired, Bina,' said the little boy.

Bina smiled at him, and Prakash said, 'Don't worry, Sonu, you'll get used to the walk. There's plenty of time.' He glanced at the old watch he'd been given by his grandfather. It needed constant winding. 'We can rest here for five or six minutes.'

They sat down on a smooth boulder and watched the clear water of the shallow stream tumbling downhill. Bina examined the old watch on Prakash's wrist. The glass was badly scratched and she could barely make out the figures on the dial. 'Are you sure it still gives the right time?' she asked.

'Well, it loses five minutes every day, so I put it ten minutes forward at night. That means by morning it's quite accurate! Even our teacher, Mr Mani, asks me for the time. If he doesn't ask, I tell him! The clock in our classroom keeps stopping.'

They removed their shoes and let the cold mountain water run over their feet. Bina was the same age as Prakash. She had pink cheeks, soft brown eyes, and hair that was just beginning to lose its natural curls. Hers was a gentle face, but a determined little chin showed that she could be a strong person. Sonu, her younger brother, was ten. He was a thin boy who had been sickly as a child but was now beginning to fill out. Although he did not look very athletic, he could run like the wind.

Bina had been going to school in her own village of Koli, on the other side of the mountain. But it had been a Primary School, finishing at Class Five. Now, in order to study in the Sixth, she would have to walk several miles every day to Nauti, where there was a High School going up to the Eighth. It had een decided that Sonu would also shift to the ew school, to give Bina company. Prakash, their eighbour in Koli, was already a pupil at the Nauti chool. His mischievous nature, which sometimes ot him into trouble, had resulted in his having to peat a year.

But this didn't seem to bother him. 'What's the urry?' he had told his indignant parents. 'You're not ending me to a foreign land when I finish school. nd our cows aren't running away, are they?'

'You would prefer to look after the cows, wouldn't ou?' asked Bina, as they got up to continue their alk.

'Oh, school's all right. Wait till you see old Mr ani. He always gets our names mixed up, as well s the subjects he's supposed to be teaching. At ut last lesson, instead of maths, he gave us a eography lesson!'

'More fun than maths,' said Bina.

'Yes, but there's a new teacher this year. She's ery young, they say, just out of college. I wonder hat she'll be like.'

Bina walked faster and Sonu had some trouble eeping up with them. She was excited about the new chool and the prospect of different surroundings. he had seldom been outside her own village, with s small school and single ration shop. The day's routine never varied – helping her mother in th fields or with household tasks like fetching wate from the spring or cutting grass and fodder for th cattle. Her father, who was a soldier, was away fo nine months in the year and Sonu was still too smal for the heavier tasks.

As they neared Nauti village, they were joined b other children coming from different directions. Eve where there were no major roads, the mountain were full of little lanes and short cuts. Like a gam of snakes and ladders, these narrow paths zigzagge around the hills and villages, cutting through field and crossing narrow ravines until they came togethe to form a fairly busy road along which mules, cattl and goats joined the throng.

Nauti was a fairly large village, and from her a broader but dustier road started for Tehri. Ther was a small bus, several trucks and (for part of th way) a road-roller. The road hadn't been complete because the heavy diesel roller couldn't take th steep climb to Nauti. It stood on the roadside hal way up the road from Tehri.

Prakash knew almost everyone in the area, an exchanged greetings and gossip with other childre as well as with muleteers, bus-drivers, milkme and labourers working on the road. He loved tellin everyone the time, even if they weren't interested.

'It's nine o'clock,' he would announce, glancing at his wrist. 'Isn't your bus leaving today?'

'Off with you!' the bus-driver would respond, 'I'll leave when I'm ready.'

As the children approached Nauti, the small flat school buildings came into view on the outskirts of the village, fringed with a line of long-leaved pines. A small crowd had assembled on the playing field. Something unusual seemed to have happened. Prakash ran forward to see what it was all about. Bina and Sonu stood aside, waiting in a patch of sunlight near the boundary wall.

Prakash soon came running back to them. He was bubbling over with excitement.

'It's Mr Mani!' he gasped. 'He's disappeared! People are saying a leopard must have carried him off!'

2

Mr Mani wasn't really old. He was about fifty-five and was expected to retire soon. But for the children, adults over forty seemed ancient! And Mr Mani had always been a bit absent-minded, even as a young man.

He had gone out for his early morning walk, saying he'd be back by eight o'clock, in time to have his breakfast and be ready for class. He wasn't married, but his sister and her husband stayed with him. When it was past nine o'clock his sister presumed he'd stopped at a neighbour's house for breakfast

(he loved tucking into other people's breakfast) ar
that he had gone on to school from there. But whe
the school bell rang at ten o'clock, and everyone bu
Mr Mani was present, questions were asked ar
guesses were made.

No one had seen him return from his walk ar
enquiries made in the village showed that he ha
not stopped at anyone's house. For Mr Mani
disappear was puzzling; for him to disappear withou
his breakfast was extraordinary.

Then a milkman returning from the next villag
said he had seen a leopard sitting on a rock on th
outskirts of the pine forest. There had been talk
a cattle-killer in the valley, of leopards and othe
animals being displaced by the construction of
dam. But as yet no one had heard of a leopar
attacking a man. Could Mr Mani have been its fir
victim? Someone found a strip of red cloth entangle
in a blackberry bush and went running through th
village showing it to everyone. Mr Mani had bee
known to wear red pyjamas. Surely, he had bee
seized and eaten! But where were his remains? An
why had he been in his pyjamas?

Meanwhile, Bina and Sonu and the rest of th
children had followed their teachers into the scho
playground. Feeling a little lost, Bina looked aroun
for Prakash. She found herself facing a dark slende
young woman wearing spectacles, who must hav

been in her early twenties – just a little too old to be another student. She had a kind expressive face and she seemed a little concerned by all that had been happening.

Bina noticed that she had lovely hands; it was obvious that the new teacher hadn't milked cows or worked in the fields!

'You must be new here,' said the teacher, smiling at Bina. 'And is this your little brother?'

'Yes, we've come from Koli village. We were at school there.'

'It's a long walk from Koli. You didn't see any leopards, did you? Well, I'm new too. Are you in the Sixth class?'

'Sonu is in the Third. I'm in the Sixth.'

'Then I'm your new teacher. My name is Tania Ramola. Come along, let's see if we can settle down in our classroom.'

Mr Mani turned up at twelve o'clock, wondering what all the fuss was about. No, he snapped, he had not been attacked by a leopard; and yes, he had lost his pyjamas and would someone kindly return them to him?

'How did you lose your pyjamas, Sir?' asked Prakash.

'They were blown off the washing line!' snapped Mr Mani.

After much questioning, Mr Mani admitted that he had gone further than he had intended, and that he had lost his way coming back. He had been a bit upset because the new teacher, a slip of a girl, had been given charge of the Sixth, while he was still with the Fifth, along with that troublesome boy Prakash, who kept on reminding him of the time! The headmaster had explained that as Mr Mani was due to retire at the end of the year, the school did not wish to burden him with a senior class. But Mr Mani looked upon the whole thing as a plot to get rid of him. He glowered at Miss Ramola whenever he passed her. And when she smiled back at him, he looked the other way!

Mr Mani had been getting even more absent-minded of late – putting on his shoes without his socks, wearing his homespun waistcoat inside out, mixing up people's names, and of course, eating other people's lunches and dinners. His sister had made a special mutton broth (*pai*) for the postmaster, who was down with 'flu' and had asked Mr Mani to take it over in a thermos. When the postmaster opened the thermos, he found only a few drops of broth at the bottom – Mr Mani had drunk the rest somewhere along the way.

When sometimes Mr Mani spoke of his coming retirement, it was to describe his plans for the small field he owned just behind the house. Right now, it was full of potatoes, which did not require much looking after; but he had plans for growing dahlias, roses, French beans, and other fruits and flowers.

The next time he visited Tehri, he promised himself, he would buy some dahlia bulbs and rose cuttings. The monsoon season would be a good time to put them down. And meanwhile, his potatoes were still flourishing.

3

Bina enjoyed her first day at the new school. She felt at ease with Miss Ramola, as did most of the boys and girls in her class. Tania Ramola had been to distant towns such as Delhi and Lucknow – places they had only read about – and it was said that she had a brother who was a pilot and flew planes all over the world. Perhaps he'd fly over Nauti some day!

Most of the children had, of course, seen planes flying overhead, but none of them had seen a ship, and only a few had been in a train. Tehri mountain was far from the railway and hundreds of miles from the sea. But they all knew about the big dam that was being built at Tehri, just forty miles away.

Bina, Sonu and Prakash had company for part of the way home, but gradually the other children went off in different directions. Once they had crossed the stream, they were on their own again.

It was a steep climb all the way back to their village. Prakash had a supply of peanuts which he shared with Bina and Sonu, and at a small spring they quenched their thirst.

When they were less than a mile from home they met a postman who had finished his round of the villages in the area and was now returning to Nauti.

'Don't waste time along the way,' he told them. 'Try to get home before dark.'

'What's the hurry?' asked Prakash, glancing at his watch. 'It's only five o'clock.'

'There's a leopard around. I saw it this morning, not far from the stream. No one is sure how it got here. So don't take any chances. Get home early.'

'So there really is a leopard,' said Sonu.

They took his advice and walked faster, and Sonu forgot to complain about his aching feet.

They were home well before sunset.

There was a smell of cooking in the air and they were hungry.

'Cabbage and roti,' said Prakash gloomily. 'But I could eat anything today.' He stopped outside his small slate-roofed house, and Bina and Sonu waved him goodbye, then carried on across a couple of ploughed fields until they reached their small stone house.

'Stuffed tomatoes,' said Sonu, sniffing just outside the front door.

'And lemon pickle,' said Bina, who had helped cut, sun and salt the lemons a month previously.

Their mother was lighting the kitchen stove. They greeted her with great hugs and demands for an immediate dinner. She was a good cook who could make even the simplest of dishes taste delicious. Her favourite saying was, 'Home-made *pai* is better than chicken soup in Delhi,' and Bina and Sonu had to agree.

Electricity had yet to reach their village, and they took their meal by the light of a kerosene lamp. After the meal, Sonu settled down to do a little homework, while Bina stepped outside to look at the stars.

Across the fields, someone was playing a flute. 'It must be Prakash,' thought Bina. 'He always breaks off on the high notes.' But the flute music was simple and appealing, and she began singing softly to herself in the dark.

4

Mr Mani was having trouble with the porcupines. They had been getting into his garden at night and digging up and eating his potatoes. From his bedroom window – left open, now that the mild-April weather had arrived – he could listen to them enjoying the vegetables he had worked hard to grow. Scrunch,

scrunch! *Katar, katar*, as their sharp teeth sliced through the largest and juiciest of potatoes. For Mr Mani it was as though they were biting through his own flesh. And the sound of them digging industriously as they rooted up those healthy, leafy plants, made him tremble with rage and indignation. The unfairness of it all!

Yes, Mr Mani hated porcupines. He prayed for their destruction, their removal from the face of the earth. But, as his friends were quick to point out, 'Bhagwan protected porcupines too,' and in any case you could never see the creatures or catch them, they were completely nocturnal.

Mr Mani got out of bed every night, torch in one hand, a stout stick in the other, but as soon as he stepped into the garden the crunching and digging stopped and he was greeted by the most infuriating of silences. He would grope around in the dark, swinging wildly with the stick, but not a single porcupine was to be seen or heard. As soon as he was back in bed – the sounds would start all over again. Scrunch, scrunch, *katar, katar*...

Mr Mani came to his class tired and dishevelled, with rings beneath his eyes and a permanent frown on his face. It took some time for his pupils to discover the reason for his misery, but when they did, they felt sorry for their teacher and took to discussing ways and means of saving his potatoes from the porcupines.

It was Prakash who came up with the idea of a moat or waterditch. 'Porcupines don't like water,' he said knowledgeably.

'How do you know?' asked one of his friends.

'Throw water on one and see how it runs! They don't like getting their quills wet.'

There was no one who could disprove Prakash's theory, and the class fell in with the idea of building a moat, especially as it meant getting most of the day off.

'Anything to make Mr Mani happy,' said the headmaster, and the rest of the school watched with envy as the pupils of Class Five, armed with spades and shovels collected from all parts of the village, took up their positions around Mr Mani's potato field and began digging a ditch.

By evening the moat was ready, but it was still dry and the porcupines got in again that night and had a great feast.

'At this rate,' said Mr Mani gloomily 'there won't be any potatoes left to save.'

But next day Prakash and the other boys and girls managed to divert the water from a stream that flowed past the village. They had the satisfaction of watching it flow gently into the ditch. Everyone went home in a good mood. By nightfall, the ditch had overflowed, the potato field was flooded, and Mr Mani found himself trapped inside his house.

But Prakash and his friends had won the day. The porcupines stayed away that night!

A month had passed, and wild violets, daisies and buttercups now sprinkled the hill slopes, and on her way to school Bina gathered enough to make a little posy. The bunch of flowers fitted easily into an old ink-well. Miss Ramola was delighted to find this little display in the middle of her desk.

'Who put these here?' she asked in surprise.

Bina kept quiet, and the rest of the class smiled secretively. After that, they took turns bringing flowers for the classroom.

On her long walks to school and home again, Bina became aware that April was the month of new leaves. The oak leaves were bright green above and silver beneath, and when they rippled in the breeze they were like clouds of silvery green. The path was strewn with old leaves, dry and crackly. Sonu loved kicking them around.

Clouds of white butterflies floated across the stream. Sonu was chasing a butterfly when he stumbled over something dark and repulsive. He went sprawling on the grass. When he got to his feet, he looked down at the remains of a small animal.

'Bina! Prakash! Come quickly!' he shouted.

It was part of a sheep, killed some days earlier by a much larger animal.

'Only a leopard could have done this,' said Prakash.

'Let's get away, then,' said Sonu. 'It might still be around!'

'No, there's nothing left to eat. The leopard will be hunting elsewhere by now. Perhaps it's moved on to the next valley.'

'Still, I'm frightened,' said Sonu. 'There may be more leopards!'

Bina took him by the hand. 'Leopards don't attack humans!' she said.

'They will, if they get a taste for people!' insisted Prakash.

'Well, this one hasn't attacked any people as yet,' said Bina, although she couldn't be sure. Hadn't there been rumours of a leopard attacking some workers near the dam? But she did not want Sonu to feel afraid, so she did not mention the story. All she said was, 'It has probably come here because of all the activity near the dam.'

All the same, they hurried home. And for a few days, whenever they reached the stream, they crossed over very quickly, unwilling to linger too long at that lovely spot.

5

A few days later, a school party was on its way to Tehri to see the new dam that was being built.

Miss Ramola had arranged to take her class, and Mr Mani, not wishing to be left out, insisted on taking his class as well. That meant there were about fifty boys and girls taking part in the outing. The little bus could only take thirty. A friendly truck-driver agreed to take some children if they were prepared to sit on sacks of potatoes. And Prakash persuaded the owner of the diesel-roller to turn it round and head it back to Tehri – with him and a couple of friends up on the driving seat.

Prakash's small group set off at sunrise, as they had to walk some distance in order to reach the stranded road-roller. The bus left at 9 a.m. with Miss Ramola and her class, and Mr Mani and some of his pupils. The truck was to follow later.

It was Bina's first visit to a large town and her first bus ride.

The sharp curves along the winding, downhill road made several children feel sick. The bus-driver seemed to be in a tearing hurry. He took them along at rolling, rollicking speed, which made Bina feel quite giddy. She rested her head on her arms and refused to look out of the window. Hairpin bends and cliff edges, pine forests and snowcapped peaks, all swept past her, but she felt too ill to want to look at anything. It was just as well – those sudden drops, hundreds of feet to the valley below, were quite frightening. Bina began to wish that she hadn't come – or that she had joined Prakash on the road-roller instead!

Miss Ramola and Mr Mani didn't seem to notice the lurching and groaning of the old bus. They had made this journey many times. They were busy arguing about the advantages and disadvantages of large dams – an argument that was to continue on and off for much of the day; sometimes in Hindi, sometimes in English, sometimes in the local dialect!

Meanwhile, Prakash and his friends had reached the roller. The driver hadn't turned up, but they managed to reverse it and get it going in the direction of Tehri. They were soon overtaken by both the bus and the truck but kept moving along at a steady chug. Prakash spotted Bina at the window of the bus and waved cheerfully. She responded feebly.

Bina felt better when the road levelled out near Tehri. As they crossed an old bridge over the wide river, they were startled by a loud bang which made the bus shudder. A cloud of dust rose above the town.

'They're blasting the mountain,' said Miss Ramola.

'End of a mountain,' said Mr Mani mournfully.

While they were drinking cups of tea at the bus stop, waiting for the potato truck and the road-roller, Miss Ramola and Mr Mani continued their argument about the dam. Miss Ramola maintained that it would bring electric power and water for irrigation to large areas of the country, including the surrounding area. Mr Mani declared that it was a menace, as it was situated in an earthquake zone. There would be a terrible disaster if the dam burst! Bina found it all very confusing. And what about the animals in the area, she wondered, what would happen to them?

The argument was becoming quite heated when the potato truck arrived. There was no sign of the road-roller, so it was decided that Mr Mani should wait for Prakash and his friends while Miss Ramola's group went ahead.

Some eight or nine miles before Tehri the road-roller had broken down, and Prakash and his friends were forced to walk. They had not gone far, however, when a mule train came along – five or six mules that had been delivering sacks of grain in Nauti. A boy rode on the first mule, but the others had no loads.

'Can you give us a ride to Tehri?' called Prakash.

'Make yourselves comfortable,' said the boy.

There were no saddles, only gunny sacks strapped on to the mules with rope. They had a rough but jolly ride down to the Tehri bus stop. None of them ad ever ridden mules; but they had saved at least n hour on the road.

Looking around the bus stop for the rest of the arty, they could find no one from their school. And Ir Mani, who should have been waiting for them, ad vanished.

6

ania Ramola and her group had taken the steep oad to the hill above Tehri. Half-an-hour's climbing rought them to a little plateau which overlooked ne town, the river and the dam-site.

The earthworks for the dam were only just coming p, but a wide tunnel had been bored through the nountain to divert the river into another channel. own below, the old town was still spread out cross the valley and from a distance it looked quite harming and picturesque.

'Will the whole town be swallowed up by the vaters of the dam?' asked Bina.

'Yes, all of it,' said Miss Ramola. 'The clock tower nd the old palace. The long bazaar, and the temples, ne schools and the jail, and hundreds of houses, or many miles up the valley. All those people will ave to go – thousands of them! Of course, they'll e resettled elsewhere.'

'But the town's been here for hundreds of years,' aid Bina. 'They were quite happy without the dam, veren't they?'

'I suppose they were. But the dam isn't jus
for them – it's for the millions who live furthe
downstream, across the plains.'

'And it doesn't matter what happens to thi
place?'

'The local people will be given new homes
somewhere else.' Miss Ramola found herself on th
defensive and decided to change the subject. 'Everyon
must be hungry. It's time we had our lunch.'

Bina kept quiet. She didn't think the local peopl
would want to go away. And it was a good thing, sh
mused, that there was only a small stream and no
a big river running past her village. To be uproote
like this – a town and hundreds of villages – and pu
down somewhere on the hot, dusty plains – seeme
to her unbearable.

'Well, I'm glad I don't live in Tehri,' she said.

She did not know it, but all the animals and mos
of the birds had already left the area. The leopar
had been among them.

They walked through the colourful, crowded bazaar
where fruit-sellers did business beside silversmiths
and pavement vendors sold everything from umbrella
to glass bangles. Sparrows attacked sacks of grain
monkeys made off with bananas, and stray cows an
dogs rummaged in refuse bins, but nobody took an
notice. Music blared from radios. Buses blew thei

orns. Sonu bought a whistle to add to the general in, but Miss Ramola told him to put it away. Bina ad kept ten rupees aside, and now she used it to uy a cotton head-scarf for her mother.

As they were about to enter a small restaurant or a meal, they were joined by Prakash and his ompanions; but of Mr Mani there was still no ign.

'He must have met one of his relatives,' said Prakash. 'He has relatives everywhere.'

After a simple meal of rice and lentils, they walked the length of the bazaar without seeing Mr Mani. At last, when they were about to give up the search, they saw him emerge from a by-lane, a large sack slung over his shoulder.

'Sir, where have you been?' asked Prakash. 'We have been looking for you everywhere.'

On Mr Mani's face was a look of triumph.

'Help me with this bag,' he said breathlessly.

'You've bought more potatoes, sir,' said Prakash.

'Not potatoes, boy. Dahlia bulbs!'

7

It was dark by the time they were all back in Nauti. Mr Mani had refused to be separated from his sack of dahlia bulbs, and had been forced to sit in the back of the truck with Prakash and most of the boys.

Bina did not feel so ill on the return journey. Goin uphill was definitely better than going downhill! Bu by the time the bus reached Nauti it was too lat for most of the children to walk back to the mor distant villages. The boys were put up in differen homes, while the girls were given beds in the schoo verandah.

The night was warm and still. Large moth fluttered around the single bulb that lit the verandah Counting moths, Sonu soon fell asleep. But Bina stayed awake for some time, listening to the sound of the night. A nightjar went *tonk-tonk* in the bushes, and somewhere in the forest an owl hooted softly. The sharp call of a barking-deer travelled up the valley, from the direction of the stream. Jackals kept howling. It seemed that there were more of them than ever before.

Bina was not the only one to hear the barking-deer. The leopard, stretched full length on a rocky ledge, heard it too. The leopard raised its head and then got up slowly. The deer was its natural prey. But there weren't many left, and that was why the leopard, robbed of its forest by the dam, had taken to attacking dogs and cattle near the villages.

As the cry of the barking-deer sounded nearer, the leopard left its look-out point and moved swiftly through the shadows towards the stream.

8

In early June the hills were dry and dusty, and forest fires broke out, destroying shrubs and trees, killing birds and small animals. The resin in the pines made these trees burn more fiercely, and the wind would take sparks from the trees and carry them into the dry grass and leaves, so that new fires would spring up before the old ones had died out. Fortunately, Bina's village was not in the pine belt; the fires did not reach it. But Nauti was surrounded by a fire that raged for three days, and the children had to stay away from school.

And then, towards the end of June, the monsoon rains arrived and there was an end to forest fires. The monsoon lasts three months and the lower Himalayas would be drenched in rain, mist and cloud for the next three months.

The first rain arrived while Bina, Prakash and Sonu were returning home from school. Those first few drops on the dusty path made them cry out with excitement. Then the rain grew heavier and a wonderful aroma rose from the earth.

'The best smell in the world!' exclaimed Bina.

Everything suddenly came to life. The grass, the crops, the trees, the birds. Even the leaves of the trees glistened and looked new.

That first wet weekend, Bina and Sonu helped their mother plant beans, maize and cucumbers.

Sometimes, when the rain was very heavy, they had to run indoors. Otherwise they worked in the rain the soft mud clinging to their bare legs.

Prakash now owned a black dog with one ear up and one ear down. The dog ran around getting in everyone's way, barking at cows, goats, hens and humans, without frightening any of them. Prakash said it was a very clever dog, but no one else seemed to think so. Prakash also said it would protect the village from the leopard, but others said the dog would be the first to be taken – he'd run straight into the jaws of Mr Spots!

In Nauti, Tania Ramola was trying to find a dry spot in the quarters she'd been given. It was an old building and the roof was leaking in several places. Mugs and buckets were scattered about the floor in order to catch the drip.

Mr Mani had dug up all his potatoes and presented them to the friends and neighbours who had given him lunches and dinners. He was having the time of his life, planting dahlia bulbs all over his garden.

'I'll have a field of many-coloured dahlias!' he announced. 'Just wait till the end of August!'

'Watch out for those porcupines,' warned his sister. 'They eat dahlia bulbs too!'

Mr Mani made an inspection tour of his moat, no longer in flood, and found everything in good order. Prakash had done his job well.

Now, when the children crossed the stream, they found that the water-level had risen by about a foot. Small cascades had turned into waterfalls. Ferns had sprung up on the banks. Frogs chanted.

Prakash and his dog dashed across the stream. Bina and Sonu followed more cautiously. The current was much stronger now and the water was almost up to their knees. Once they had crossed the stream, they hurried along the path, anxious not to be caught in a sudden downpour.

By the time they reached school, each of them had two or three leeches clinging to their legs. They had to use salt to remove them. The leeches were the most troublesome part of the rainy season. Even the leopard did not like them. It could not lie in the long grass without getting leeches on its paws and face.

One day, when Bina, Prakash and Sonu were about to cross the stream they heard a low rumble, which grew louder every second. Looking up at the opposite hill, they saw several trees shudder, tilt outwards and begin to fall. Earth and rocks bulged out from the mountain, then came crashing down into the ravine.

'Landslide!' shouted Sonu.

'It's carried away the path,' said Bina. 'Don't go any further.'

There was a tremendous roar as more rocks, trees and bushes fell away and crashed down the hillside.

Prakash's dog, who had gone ahead, came running back, tail between his legs.

They remained rooted to the spot until the rocks had stopped falling and the dust had settled. Birds circled the area, calling wildly. A frightened barking-deer ran past them.

'We can't go to school now,' said Prakash. 'There's no way around.'

They turned and trudged home through the gathering mist.

In Koli, Prakash's parents had heard the roar of the landslide. They were setting out in search of the children when they saw them emerge from the mist, waving cheerfully.

9

They had to miss school for another three days, and Bina was afraid they might not be able to take their final exams. Although Prakash was not really troubled at the thought of missing exams, he did not like feeling helpless just because their path had been swept away. So he explored the hillside until he found a goat-track going around the mountain. It joined up with another path near Nauti. This made their walk longer by a mile, but Bina did not mind. It was much cooler now that the rains were in full swing.

The only trouble with the new route was that it passed close to the leopard's lair. The animal had made this area its own since being forced to leave the dam area.

One day Prakash's dog ran ahead of them, barking furiously. Then he ran back, whimpering.

'He's always running away from something,' observed Sonu. But a minute later he understood the reason for the dog's fear.

They rounded a bend and Sonu saw the leopard standing in their way. They were struck dumb – too terrified to run. It was a strong, sinewy creature. A low growl rose from its throat. It seemed ready to spring.

They stood perfectly still, afraid to move or say a word. And the leopard must have been equally surprised. It stared at them for a few seconds, then bounded across the path and into the oak forest.

Sonu was shaking. Bina could hear her heart hammering. Prakash could only stammer: 'Did you see the way he sprang? Wasn't he beautiful?'

He forgot to look at his watch for the rest of the day.

A few days later Sonu stopped and pointed to a large outcrop of rock on the next hill.

The leopard stood far above them, outlined against the sky. It looked strong, majestic. Standing beside it were two young cubs.

'Look at those little ones!' exclaimed Sonu.

'So it's a female, not a male,' said Prakash.

'That's why she was killing so often,' said Bina. 'She had to feed her cubs too.'

They remained still for several minutes, gazing up at the leopard and her cubs. The leopard family took no notice of them.

'She knows we are here,' said Prakash, 'but she doesn't care. She knows we won't harm them.'

'We are cubs too!' said Sonu.

'Yes,' said Bina. 'And there's still plenty of space for all of us. Even when the dam is ready there will still be room for leopards and humans.'

10

The school exams were over. The rains were nearly over too. The landslide had been cleared, and Bina, Prakash and Sonu were once again crossing the stream.

There was a chill in the air, for it was the end of September.

Prakash had learnt to play the flute quite well, and he played on the way to school and then again on the way home. As a result he did not look at his watch so often.

One morning they found a small crowd in front of Mr Mani's house.

'What could have happened?' wondered Bina. 'I hope he hasn't got lost again.'

'Maybe he's sick,' said Sonu.

'Maybe it's the porcupines,' said Prakash.

But it was none of these things.

Mr Mani's first dahlia was in bloom, and half the village had turned out to look at it! It was a huge red double dahlia, so heavy that it had to be supported with sticks. No one had ever seen such a magnificent flower!

Mr Mani was a happy man. And his mood only improved over the coming week, as more and more dahlias flowered – crimson, yellow, purple, mauve, white – button dahlias, pompom dahlias, spotted dahlias, striped dahlias... Mr Mani had them all! A dahlia even turned up on Tania Romola's desk – he got on quite well with her now – and another brightened up the headmaster's study.

A week later, on their way home – it was almost the last day of the school term – Bina, Prakash and Sonu talked about what they might do when they grew up.

'I think I'll become a teacher,' said Bina. 'I'll teach children about animals and birds, and trees and flowers.'

'Better than maths!' said Prakash.

'I'll be a pilot,' said Sonu. 'I want to fly a plane like Miss Ramola's brother.'

'And what about you, Prakash?' asked Bina.

Prakash just smiled and said, 'Maybe I'll be a flute-player,' and he put the flute to he lips and played a sweet melody.

'Well, the world needs flute-players too,' said Bina, as they fell into step beside him.

The leopard had been stalking a barking-deer. She paused when she heard the flute and the voices of the children. Her own young ones were growing quickly, but the girl and the two boys did not look much older.

They had started singing their favourite song again.

Five more miles to go!
We climb through rain and snow,
A river to cross...
A mountain to pass...
Now we've four more miles to go!

The leopard waited until they had passed, before returning to the trail of the barking-deer.

The Wind on Haunted Hill

Whoo, whoo, whoo, cried the wind as it swept down from the Himalayan snows. It hurried over the hills and passed and hummed and moaned through the tall pines and deodars. There was little on Haunted Hill to stop the wind – only a few stunted trees and bushes and the ruins of a small settlement.

On the slopes of the next hill was a village. People kept large stones on their tin roofs to prevent them from being blown off. There was nearly always a strong wind in these parts. Three children were spreading clothes out to dry on a low stone wall, putting a stone on each piece.

Eleven-year-old Usha, dark-haired and rose-cheeked, struggled with her grandfather's long, loose shirt. Her younger brother, Suresh, was doing his best to hold down a bedsheet, while Usha's friend, Binya, a slightly older girl, helped.

Once everything was firmly held down by stones, they climbed up on the flat rocks and sat there sunbathing and staring across the fields at the ruins on Haunted Hill.

'I must go to the bazaar today,' said Usha.

'I wish I could come too,' said Binya. 'But I have to help with the cows.'

'I can come!' said eight-year-old Suresh. He was always ready to visit the bazaar, which was three miles away, on the other side of the hill.

'No, you can't,' said Usha. 'You must help Grandfather chop wood.'

'Won't you feel scared returning alone?' he asked. 'There are ghosts on Haunted Hill!'

'I'll be back before dark. Ghosts don't appear during the day.'

'Are there lots of ghosts in the ruins?' asked Binya.

'Grandfather says so. He says that over a hundred years ago, some Britishers lived on the hill. But the settlement was always being struck by lightning, so they moved away.'

'But if they left, why is the place visited by ghosts?'

'Because – Grandfather says – during a terrible storm, one of the houses was hit by lightning, and everyone in it was killed. Even the children.'

'How many children?'

'Two. A boy and his sister. Grandfather saw them playing there in the moonlight.'

'Wasn't he frightened?'

'No. Old people don't mind ghosts.'

Usha set out for the bazaar at two in the afternoon. It was about an hour's walk. The path went through yellow fields of flowering mustard, then along the saddle of the hill, and up, straight through the ruins. Usha had often gone that way to shop at the bazaar or to see her aunt, who lived in the town nearby.

Wild flowers bloomed on the crumbling walls of the ruins, and a wild plum tree grew straight out of the floor of what had once been a hall. It was covered with soft, white blossoms. Lizards scuttled over the stones, while a whistling thrush, its deep purple plumage glistening in the sunshine, sat on a window-sill and sang its heart out.

Usha sang too, as she skipped lightly along the path, which dipped steeply down to the valley and led to the little town with its quaint bazaar.

Moving leisurely, Usha bought spices, sugar and matches. With the two rupees she had saved from her pocket-money, she chose a necklace of amber-coloured beads for herself and some marbles for Suresh. Then she had her mother's slippers repaired at a cobbler's shop.

Finally, Usha went to visit Aunt Lakshmi at her flat above the shops. They were talking and drinking cups of hot, sweet tea when Usha realised that dark clouds had gathered over the mountains. She quickly picked up her things, said goodbye to her aunt, and set out for the village.

Strangely, the wind had dropped. The trees were still, the crickets silent. The crows flew round in circles, then settled on an oak tree.

'I must get home before dark,' thought Usha, hurrying along the path.

But the sky had darkened and a deep rumble echoed over the hills. Usha felt the first heavy drop of rain hit her cheek. Holding the shopping bag close to her body, she quickened her pace until she was almost running. The raindrops were coming down faster now – cold, stinging pellets of rain. A flash of lightning sharply outlined the ruins on the hill, and then all was dark again. Night had fallen.

'I'll have to shelter in the ruins,' Usha thought and began to run. Suddenly the wind sprang up again, but she did not have to fight it. It was behind her now, helping her along, up the steep path and on to the brow of the hill. There was another flash of lightning, followed by a peal of thunder. The ruins loomed before her, grim and forbidding.

Usha remembered part of an old roof that would give some shelter. It would be better than trying to go on. In the dark, with the howling wind, she might stray off the path and fall over the edge of the cliff.

Whoo, whoo, whoo, howled the wind. Usha saw the wild plum tree swaying, its foliage thrashing against the ground. She found her way into the ruins, helped by the constant flicker of lightning. Usha placed her hands flat against a stone wall and moved sideways, hoping to reach the sheltered corner. Suddenly, her hand touched something soft and furry, and she gave a startled cry. Her cry was answered by another – half snarl, half screech – as something leapt away in the darkness.

With a sigh of relief Usha realised that it was the cat that lived in the ruins. For a moment she had been frightened, but now she moved quickly along the wall until she heard the rain drumming on a remnant of a tin roof. Crouched in a corner, she found some shelter. But the tin sheet groaned and clattered as if it would sail away any moment.

Usha remembered that across this empty room stood an old fireplace. Perhaps it would be drier there under the blocked chimney. But she would not attempt to find it just now – she might lose her way altogether.

Her clothes were soaked and water streamed down from her hair, forming a puddle at her feet. She thought she heard a faint cry – the cat again, or an owl? Then the storm blotted out all other sounds.

There had been no time to think of ghosts, but now that she was settled in one place, Usha remembered Grandfather's story about the lightning-blasted ruins. She hoped and prayed that lightning would not strike her.

Thunder boomed over the hills, and the lightning came quicker now. Then there was a bigger flash, and for a moment the entire ruin was lit up. A streak of blue sizzled along the floor of the building. Usha was staring straight ahead, and, as the opposite wall lit up, she saw, crouching in front of the unused fireplace, two small figures – children!

The ghostly figures seemed to look up and stare back at Usha. And then everything was dark again.

Usha's heart was in her mouth. She had seen without doubt, two ghosts on the other side of the room. She wasn't going to remain in the ruins one minute longer.

She ran towards the big gap in the wall through which she had entered. She was halfway across the open space when something – someone – fell against her. Usha stumbled, got up, and again bumped into something. She gave a frightened scream. Someone else screamed. And then there was a shout, a boy's shout, and Usha instantly recognised the voice.

'Suresh!'

'Usha!'

'Binya!'

They fell into each other's arms, so surprised and relieved that all they could do was laugh and giggle and repeat each other's names.

Then Usha said, 'I thought you were ghosts.'

'We thought you were a ghost,' said Suresh.

'Come back under the roof,' said Usha.

They huddled together in the corner, chattering with excitement and relief.

'When it grew dark, we came looking for you,' said Binya. 'And then the storm broke.'

'Shall we run back together?' asked Usha. 'I don't want to stay here any longer.'

'We'll have to wait,' said Binya. 'The path has fallen away at one place. It won't be safe in the dark, in all this rain.'

'We'll have to wait till morning,' said Suresh, 'and I'm so hungry!'

The storm continued, but they were not afraid now. They gave each other warmth and confidence. Even the ruins did not seem so forbidding.

After an hour the rain stopped, and the thunder grew more distant.

Towards dawn the whistling thrush began to sing. Its sweet, broken notes flooded the ruins with music. As the sky grew lighter, they saw that the plum tree stood upright again, though it had lost all its blossoms.

'Let's go,' said Usha.

Outside the ruins, walking along the brow of the hill, they watched the sky grow pink. When they were some distance away, Usha looked back and said, 'Can you see something behind the wall? It's like a hand waving.'

'It's just the top of the plum tree,' said Binya.

'Goodbye, goodbye...' They heard voices.

'Who said "goodbye"?' asked Usha.

'Not I,' said Suresh.

'Nor I,' said Binya.

'I heard someone calling,' said Usha.

'It's only the wind,' assured Binya.

Usha looked back at the ruins. The sun had come up and was touching the top of the wall.

'Come on,' said Suresh. 'I'm *hungry*.'

They hurried along the path to the village.

'Goodbye, goodbye...' Usha heard them calling. Or was it just the wind?

Romi and the Wildfire

1

As Romi was about to mount his bicycle, he saw smoke rising from behind the distant line of trees.

'It looks like a forest fire,' said Prem, his friend and classmate.

'It's well to the east,' said Romi. 'Nowhere near the road.'

'There's a strong wind,' said Prem, looking at the dry leaves swirling across the road.

It was the middle of May, and it hadn't rained in the Terai for several weeks. The grass was brown, the leaves of the trees covered with dust. Even though it was getting on to six o'clock in the evening, the boys' shirts were damp with sweat.

'It will be getting dark soon,' said Prem. 'You'd better spend the night at my house.'

'No, I said I'd be home tonight. My father isn't keeping well. The doctor has given me some tablets for him.'

'You'd better hurry, then. That fire seems to be spreading.'

'Oh, it's far off. It will take me only forty minutes to ride through the forest. 'Bye, Prem – see you tomorrow!'

Romi mounted his bicycle and pedalled off down the main road of the village, scattering stray hens, stray dogs and stray villagers.

'Hey, look where you're going!' shouted an angry villager, leaping out of the way of the oncoming bicycle. 'Do you think you own the road?'

'Of course I own it,' called Romi cheerfully, and cycled on.

His own village lay about seven miles distant, on the other side of the forest; but there was only a primary school in his village, and Romi was now in High School. His father, who was a fairly wealthy sugarcane farmer, had only recently bought him the bicycle. Romi didn't care too much for school and felt there weren't enough holidays; but he enjoyed the long rides, and he got on well with his classmates.

He might have stayed the night with Prem had it not been for the tablets which the Vaid – the village doctor – had given him for his father.

Romi's father was having back trouble, and the medicine had been specially prepared from local herbs.

Having been given such a fine bicycle, Romi felt that the least he could do in return was to get those tablets to his father as early as possible.

He put his head down and rode swiftly out of the village. Ahead of him, the smoke rose from the burning forest and the sky glowed red.

2

He had soon left the village far behind. There was a slight climb, and Romi had to push harder on the pedals to get over the rise. Once over the top, the road went winding down to the edge of the sub-tropical forest.

This was the part Romi enjoyed most. He relaxed, stopped pedalling, and allowed the bicycle to glide gently down the slope. Soon the wind was rushing past him, blowing his hair about his face and making his shirt billow out behind. He burst into song.

A dog from the village ran beside him, barking furiously. Romi shouted to the dog, encouraging him in the race.

Then the road straightened out, and Romi began pedalling again.

The dog, seeing the forest ahead, turned back to the village. It was afraid of the forest.

The smoke was thicker now, and Romi caught the smell of burning timber. But ahead of him the road was clear. He rode on.

It was a rough, dusty road, cut straight through the forest. Tall trees grew on either side, cutting off the last of the daylight. But the spreading glow of the fire on the right lit up the road, and giant tree-shadows danced before the boy on the bicycle.

Usually the road was deserted. This evening it was alive with wild creatures fleeing from the forest fire.

The first animal that Romi saw was a hare, leaping across the road in front of him. It was followed by several more hares. Then a band of monkeys streamed across, chattering excitedly.

They'll be safe on the other side, thought Romi. The fire won't cross the road.

But it was coming closer. And realising this, Romi pedalled harder. In half-an-hour he should be out of the forest.

Suddenly, from the side of the road, several pheasants rose in the air, and with a *whoosh,* flew low across the path, just in front of the oncoming bicycle. Taken by surprise, Romi fell off. When he picked himself up and began brushing his clothes, he saw that his knee was bleeding. It wasn't a deep cut, but he allowed it to bleed a little, took out his handkerchief and bandaged his knee. Then he mounted the bicycle again.

He rode a bit slower now, because birds and animals kept coming out of the bushes.

Not only pheasants but smaller birds, too, were streaming across the road – parrots, jungle crows, owls, magpies – and the air was filled with their cries.

'Everyone's on the move,' thought Romi. It must be a really big fire.

He could see the flames now, reaching out from behind the trees on his right, and he could hear the crackling as the dry leaves caught fire. The air was hot on his face. Leaves, still alight or turning to cinders, floated past.

A herd of deer crossed the road, and Romi had to stop until they had passed. Then he mounted again and rode on; but now, for the first time, he was feeling afraid.

3

From ahead came a faint clanging sound. It wasn't an animal sound, Romi was sure of that. A fire-engine? There were no fire-engines within fifty miles.

The clanging came nearer, and Romi discovered that the noise came from a small boy who was running along the forest path, two milk-cans clattering at his side

'Teju!' called Romi, recognising the boy from a neighbouring village. 'What are you doing out here?'

'Trying to get home, of course,' said Teju, panting along beside the bicycle.

'Jump on,' said Romi, stopping for him.

Teju was only eight or nine – a couple of years younger than Romi. He had come to deliver milk to some road-workers, but the workers had left at the first signs of the fire, and Teju was hurrying home with his cans still full of milk.

He got up on the cross-bar of the bicycle, and Romi moved on again. He was quite used to carrying friends on the crossbar.

'Keep beating your milk-cans,' said Romi. 'Like that, the animals will know we are coming. My bell doesn't make enough noise. I'm going to get a *horn* for my cycle!'

'I never knew there were so many animals in the jungle,' said Teju. 'I saw a python in the middle of the road. It stretched right across!'

'What did you do?'

'Just kept running and jumped right over it!'

Teju continued to chatter but Romi's thoughts were on the fire, which was much closer now. Flames shot up from the dry grass and ran up the trunks of trees and along the branches. Smoke billowed out above the forest.

Romi's eyes were smarting and his hair and eyebrows felt scorched. He was feeling tired but he couldn't stop now, he had to get beyond the range of the fire. Another ten or fifteen minutes of steady riding would get them to the small wooden bridge that spanned the little river separating the forest from the sugarcane fields.

Once across the river, they would be safe. The fire could not touch them on the other side, because the forest ended at the river's edge. But could they get to the river in time?

4

Clang, clang, clang, went Teju's milk-cans. But the sound of the fire grew louder too.

A tall silk-cotton tree, its branches leaning across the road, had caught fire. They were almost beneath it when there was a crash and a burning branch fell to the ground a few yards in front of them.

The boys had to get off the bicycle and leave the road, forcing their way through a tangle of thorny bushes on the left, dragging and pushing at the bicycle and only returning to the road some distance ahead of the burning tree.

'We won't get out in time,' said Teju, back on the cross-bar but feeling disheartened.

'Yes, we will,' said Romi, pedalling with all his might. 'The fire hasn't crossed the road as yet.'

Even as he spoke, he saw a small flame leap up from the grass on the left. It wouldn't be long before more sparks and burning leaves were blown across the road to kindle the grass on the other side.

'Oh, look!' exclaimed Romi, bringing the bicycle to a sudden stop.

'What's wrong now?' asked Teju, rubbing his sore eyes. And then, through the smoke, he saw what was stopping them.

An elephant was standing in the middle of the road.

Teju slipped off the cross-bar, his cans rolling on the ground, bursting open and spilling their contents.

The elephant was about forty feet away. It moved about restlessly, its big ears flapping as it turned its head from side to side, wondering which way to go.

From far to the left, where the forest was still untouched, a herd of elephants moved towards the river. The leader of the herd raised his trunk and trumpeted a call. Hearing it, the elephant in the road raised its own trunk and trumpeted a reply. Then it shambled off into the forest, in the direction of the herd, leaving the way clear.

'Come, Teju, jump on!' urged Romi. 'We can't stay here much longer!'

5

Teju forgot about his milk-cans and pulled himself up on the cross-bar. Romi ran forward with the bicycle, to gain speed, and mounted swiftly. He kept as far as possible to the left of the road, trying to ignore the flames, the crackling, the smoke and the scorching heat.

It seemed that all the animals who could get away had done so. The exodus across the road had stopped.

'We won't stop again,' said Romi, gritting his teeth. 'Not even for an elephant!'

'We're nearly there!' said Teju. He was perking up again.

A jackal, overcome by the heat and smoke, lay in the middle of the path, either dead or unconscious. Romi did not stop. He swerved round the animal. Then he put all his strength into one final effort.

He covered the last hundred yards at top speed, and then they were out of the forest, free-wheeling down the sloping road to the river.

'Look!' shouted Teju. 'The bridge is on fire!'

Burning embers had floated down on to the small wooden bridge, and the dry, ancient timber had quickly caught fire. It was now burning fiercely.

Romi did not hesitate. He left the road, riding the bicycle over sand and pebbles. Then with a rush they went down the river-bank and into the water.

The next thing they knew they were splashing around, trying to find each other in the darkness.

'Help!' cried Teju. 'I'm drowning!'

6

'Don't be silly,' said Romi. 'The water isn't deep – it's only up to the knees. Come here and grab hold of me.'

Teju splashed across and grabbed Romi by the belt.

'The water's so cold,' he said, his teeth chattering.

'Do you want to go back and warm yourself?' asked Romi. 'Some people are never satisfied. Come on, help me get the bicycle up. It's down here, just where we are standing.'

Together they managed to heave the bicycle out of the water and stand it upright.

'Now sit on it,' said Romi. 'I'll push you across.'

'We'll be swept away,' said Teju.

'No, we won't. There's not much water in the river at this time of the year. But the current is quite strong in the middle, so sit still. All right?'

'All right,' said Teju nervously.

Romi began guiding the bicycle across the river, one hand on the seat and one hand on the handlebar. The river was shallow and sluggish in midsummer;

even so, it was quite swift in the middle. But having got safely out of the burning forest, Romi was in no mood to let a little river defeat him.

He kicked off his shoes, knowing they would be lost; and then gripping the smooth stones of the river-bed with his toes, he concentrated on keeping his balance and getting the bicycle and Teju through the middle of the stream. The water here came up to his waist, and the current would have been too strong for Teju. But when they reached the shallows, Teju got down and helped Romi push the bicycle.

They reached the opposite bank, and sank down on the grass.

'We can rest now,' said Romi. 'But not all night – I've got some medicine to give to my father.' He felt in his pockets and found that the tablets in their envelope, had turned into a soggy mess. 'Oh well, he had to take them with water anyway,' he said.

They watched the fire as it continued to spread through the forest. It had crossed the road down which they had come. The sky was a bright red, and the river reflected the colour of the sky.

Several elephants had found their way down to the river. They were cooling off by spraying water on each other with their trunks. Further downstream there were deer and other animals.

Romi and Teju looked at each other in the glow from the fire. They hadn't known each other very well before. But now they felt they had been friends for years.

'What are you thinking about?' asked Teju.

'I'm thinking,' said Romi, 'that even if the fire is out in a day or two, it will be a long time before the bridge is repaired. So it will be a nice long holiday from school!'

'But you can walk across the river,' said Teju. 'You just did it.'

'Impossible,' said Romi. 'It's much too swift.'

Tiger My Friend

1

On the left bank of the river Ganges, where it flows out from the Himalayan foothills, is a ong stretch of heavy forest. There are villages on he fringe of the forest, inhabited by farmers and erdsmen. Big-game hunters came to the area for nany years, and as a result the animals had been etting fewer. The trees, too, had been disappearing lowly; and as the animals lost their food and shelter, hey moved further into the foothills.

There was a time when this forest had provided home for some thirty to forty tigers, but men in search of skins and trophies had shot them all and now there remained only one old tiger in the jungle. The hunters had tried to get him, too, bu he was a wise and crafty tiger, who knew the ways of man, and so far he had survived all attempts or his life.

Although the tiger had passed the prime of his life, he had lost none of his majesty. His muscles rippled beneath the golden yellow of his coat, and he walked through the long grass with the confidence o one who knew that he was still a king, although his subjects were fewer. His great head pushed through the foliage, and it was only his tail, swinging high that sometimes showed above the sea of grass.

He was heading for water, the water of a large marsh, where he sometimes went to drink or coo off. The marsh was usually deserted except when the buffaloes from a nearby village were brought there to bathe or wallow in the muddy water.

The tiger waited in the shelter of a rock, his ears pricked for any unfamiliar sound. He knew that i was here that hunters sometimes waited for him with guns.

He walked into the water, amongst the water lilies, and drank slowly. He was seldom in a hurry when he ate or drank.

He raised his head and listened, one paw suspended in the air.

A strange sound had come to him on the breeze, and he was wary of strange sounds. So he moved swiftly into the shelter of the tall grass that bordered the marsh, and climbed a hillock until he reached his favourite rock. This rock was big enough to hide him and to give him shade.

The sound he had heard was only a flute, sounding thin and reedy in the forest. It belonged to Nandu, a slim brown boy who rode a buffalo. Nandu played vigorously on the flute. Chottu, a slightly smaller boy, riding another buffalo, brought up the rear of the herd.

There were eight buffaloes in the herd, which belonged to the families of Nandu and Chottu, who were cousins. Their fathers sold buffalo-milk and butter in villages further down the river.

The tiger had often seen them at the marsh, and he was not bothered by their presence. He knew the village folk would leave him alone as long as he did not attack their buffaloes. And as long as there were deer in the jungle, he would not be interested in other prey.

He decided to move on and find a cool shady place in the heart of the jungle, where he could rest during the hot afternoon and be free of the flies and mosquitoes that swarmed around the marsh. At night he would hunt.

With a lazy grunt that was half a roar, 'A-oonh!' – he got off his haunches and sauntered off into the jungle.

The gentlest of tigers' roars can be heard a mile away, and the boys, who were barely fifty yards distant, looked up immediately.

'There he goes!' said Nandu, taking the flute from his lips and pointing with it towards the hillock. 'Did you see him?'

'I saw his tail, just before he disappeared. He's a big tiger!'

'Don't' call him tiger. Call him Uncle.'

'Why?' asked Chottu.

'Because it's unlucky to call a tiger a tiger. My father told me so. But if you meet a tiger, and call him Uncle, he will leave you alone.'

'I see,' said Chottu. 'You have to make him a relative. I'll try and remember that.'

The buffaloes were now well into the march, and some of them were lying down in the mud. Buffaloes love soft wet mud and will wallow in it for hours. Nandu and Chottu were not so fond of the mud, so they went swimming in deeper water. Later, they rested in the shade of an old silk-cotton tree.

It was evening, and the twilight fading fast, when the buffalo herd finally made its way homeward, to be greeted outside the village by the barking of dogs, the gurgle of hookah-pipes, and the homely smell of cow-dung smoke.

2

The following evening, when Nandu and Chottu came home with the buffalo herd, they found a crowd of curious villagers surrounding a jeep in which sat three strangers with guns. They were hunters, and they were accompanied by servants and a large store of provisions.

They had heard that there was a tiger in the area, and they wanted to shoot it.

These men had money to spend; and, as most of the villagers were poor, they were prepared to go into the forest to make a *machaan* or tree-platform for the hunters. The platform, big enough to take the three men, was put up in the branches of a tall mahogany tree.

Nandu was told by his father to tie a goat at the foot of the tree. While these preparations were being made, Chottu slipped off and circled the area, with a plan of his own in mind. He had no wish to see the tiger killed and he had decided to give it some sort of warning. So he tied up bits and pieces of old clothing on small trees and bushes. He knew the wily old king of the jungle would keep well away from the area if he saw the bits of clothing – for where there were men's clothes, there would be men.

The vigil kept by the hunters lasted all through the night, but the tiger did not come near the tree.

Perhaps he'd got Chottu's warning; or perhaps he wasn't hungry.

It was a cold night, and it wasn't long before the hunters opened their flasks of rum. Soon they were whispering among themselves; then they were chattering so loudly that no wild animal would have come anywhere near them. By morning they were fast asleep.

They looked grumpy and shamefaced as they trudged back to the village.

'Wrong time of the year for tiger,' said the first hunter.

'Nothing left in these parts,' said the second.

'I think I've caught a cold,' said the third. And they drove away in disgust.

It was not until the beginning of the summer that something happened to alter the hunting habits of the tiger and bring him into conflict with the villagers.

There had been no rain for almost two months, and the tall jungle grass had become a sea of billowy dry yellow. Some city-dwellers, camping near the forest, had been careless while cooking and had started a forest fire. Slowly it spread into the interior, from where the acrid fumes smoked the tiger out towards the edge of the jungle. As night came on, the flames grew more vivid, the smell stronger. The tiger turned and made for the marsh, where he knew he would be safe provided he swam across to the little island in the centre.

Next morning he was on the island, which was untouched by the fire. But his surroundings had changed. The slopes of the hills were black with burnt grass, and most of the tall bamboo had disappeared. The deer and the wild pig, finding that their natural cover had gone, moved further east.

When the fire had died down and the smoke had cleared, the tiger prowled through the forest again but found no game. He drank at the marsh and settled down in a shady spot to sleep the day away.

The tiger spent four days looking for game. By that time he was so hungry that he even resorted to rooting among the dead leaves and burnt-out stumps of trees, searching for worms and beetles. This was a sad comedown for the king of the jungle. But even now he hesitated to leave the area in search of new hunting grounds, for he had a deep fear and suspicion of the unknown forests further east – forests that were fast being swept away by human habitation. He could have gone north, into the high mountains, but they did not provide him with the long grass he needed for cover.

At break of day he came to the marsh. The water was now shallow and muddy, and a green scum had spread over the top. He drank, and then lay down across his favourite rock, hoping for a deer;

but none came. He was about to get up and lope away when he heard an animal approach.

The tiger at once slipped off his rock and flattened himself on the ground, his tawny stripes merging with the dry grass.

A buffalo emerged from the jungle and came to the water. The buffalo was alone. He was a big male, and his long curved horns lay right back across his shoulders. He moved leisurely towards the water, completely unaware of the tiger's presence.

The tiger hesitated before making his charge.

It was a long time – many years – since he had killed a buffalo, and he knew instinctively that the villagers would be angry. But the pangs of hunger overcame his caution. There was no morning breeze, everything was still, and the smell of the tiger did not reach the buffalo. A monkey chattered on a nearby tree, but his warning went unheeded.

Crawling stealthily on his stomach, the tiger skirted the edge of the marsh and approached the buffalo from behind. The buffalo was standing in shallow water, drinking, when the tiger charged from the side and sank his teeth into his victim's thigh.

The buffalo staggered, but turned to fight. He snorted and lowered his horns at the tiger. But the big cat was too fast for the brave buffalo. He bit into the other leg and the buffalo crashed to the ground. Then the tiger moved in for the kill.

After resting, he began to eat. Although he had been starving for days, he could not finish the huge carcass. And so he quenched his thirst at the marsh and dragged the remains of the buffalo into the bushes, to conceal it from jackals and vultures; then he went off to find a place to sleep.

He would return to the kill when he was hungry.

3

The herdsmen were naturally very upset when they discovered that a buffalo was missing. And next day, when Nandu and Chottu came running home to say that they had found the half-eaten carcass near the marsh, the men of the village grew angry. They knew that once the tiger realised how easy it was to kill their animals, he would make a habit of doing so.

Kundan Singh, Nandu's father, who owned the buffalo, said he would go after the tiger himself.

'It's too late now,' said his wife. 'You should never have let the buffalo roam on its own.'

'He had been on his own before. This is the first time the tiger has attacked one of our animals.'

'He must have been hungry,' said Chottu.

'Well, we are hungry too,' said Kundan Singh. 'Our best buffalo – the only male in the herd. It will cost me at least two thousand rupees to buy another.'

'The tiger will kill again,' said Chottu's father. 'Many years ago there was a tiger who did the same thing. He became a cattle-killer.'

'Should we send for the hunters?'

'No, they are clumsy fools. The tiger will return to the carcass for another meal. You have a gun?'

Kundan Singh smiled proudly and, going to a cupboard, brought out a double-barrelled gun. It looked ancient!

'My father bought it from an Englishman,' he said.

'How long ago was that?'

'About the time I was born.'

'And have you ever used it?' asked Chottu's father, looking at the old gun with distrust.

'A few years ago I let it off at some bandits. Don't you remember? When I fired, they did not stop running until they had crossed the river.'

'Yes, but did you hit anyone?'

'I would have, if someone's goat hadn't got in the way.'

'We had roast meat that night,' said Nandu.

Accompanied by Chottu's father and several others, Kundan set out for the marsh, where, without shifting the buffalo's carcass – for they knew the tiger would not come near them if he suspected a trap – they made another tree-platform in the branches of a tall tree some thirty feet from the kill.

Late that evening, Kundan Singh and Chottu's father settled down for the night on their rough platform.

Several hours passed and nothing but a jackal was seen by the watchers. And then, just as the moon came up over the distant hills, the two men were startled by a low 'A-oonh', followed by a suppressed, rumbling growl.

Kundan tightened his grip on the old gun. There was complete silence for a minute or two, then the sound of stealthy footfalls on the dead leaves beneath the tree.

A moment later the tiger walked out into the moonlight and stood over his kill.

At first Kundan could do nothing. He was completely taken aback by the size of the tiger. Chottu's father had to nudge him, and then Kundan quickly put the gun to his shoulder, aimed at the tiger's head, and pressed the trigger.

The gun went off with a flash and two loud bangs, as Kundan fired both barrels. There was a tremendous roar. The tiger rushed at the tree and tried to leap into the branches. Fortunately, the platform had been built at a good height, and the tiger was unable to reach it.

He roared again and then bounded off into the forest.

'What a tiger!' exclaimed Kundan, half in fear and half in admiration.

'You missed him completely,' said Chottu's father.

'I did not,' said Kundan. 'You heard him roar! Would he have been so angry if he had not been hit?'

'Well, if you have only wounded him, he will turn into a man-eater – and where will that leave us?'

'He won't be back,' said Kundan. 'He will leave this area.'

During the next few days the tiger lay low. He did not go near the marsh except when it was very dark and he was very thirsty. The herdsmen and villagers decided that the tiger had gone away. Nandu and Chottu – usually accompanied by other village youths, and always carrying their small hand-axes – began bringing the buffaloes to the marsh again during the day; they were careful not to let any of them stray far from the herd.

But one day, while the boys were taking the herd home, one of the buffaloes lagged behind. Nandu did not realise that an animal was missing until he heard an agonised bellow behind him. He glanced over his shoulder just in time to see the tiger dragging the buffalo into a clump of bamboo. The herd sensed the danger, and the buffaloes snorted with fear as they hurried along the forest path. To urge them forward and to warn his friends, Nandu cupped his hands to his mouth and gave a yodelling call.

The buffaloes bellowed, the boys shouted, and the birds flew shrieking from the trees. Together they stampeded out of the forest. The villagers heard the thunder of hoofs, and saw the herd coming home amidst clouds of dust.

'The tiger!' called Nandu. 'He is back! He has taken another buffalo!'

'He is afraid of us no longer,' thought Chottu. And now everyone will hate him and do their best to kill him.

'Did you see where he went?' asked Kundan Singh, hurrying up to them.

'I remember the place,' said Nandu.

'Then there is no time to lose,' said Kundan. 'I will take my gun and a few men, and wait near the bridge. The rest of you must beat the jungle from this side and drive the tiger towards me. He will not escape this time, unless he swims across the river!'

4

Kundan took his men and headed for the suspension bridge over the river, while the others, guided by Nandu and Chottu, went to the spot where the tiger had seized the buffalo.

The tiger was still eating when he heard the men coming. He had not expected to be disturbed so soon.

With an angry 'Whoof!' he bounded into the jungle, and watched the men – there were some twenty of them – through a screen of leaves and tall grass.

The men carried hand drums slung from their shoulders, and some carried sticks and spears. After a hurried consultation, they strung out in a line and entered the jungle beating their drums.

The tiger did not like the noise. He went deeper into the jungle. But the men came after him, banging away on their drums and shouting at the top of their voices. They advanced singly or in pairs, but nowhere were they more than fifteen yards apart.

The tiger could easily have broken through this slowly advancing semi-circle of men – one swift blow from his paw would have felled the strongest of them – but his main object was to get away from the noise. He hated and feared the noise made by humans.

He was not a man-eater and he would not attack a man unless he was very angry or very frightened; and as yet he was neither. He had eaten well, and he would have liked to rest – but there would be no rest for him until the men ceased their tremendous clatter and din.

Nandu and Chottu kept close to their elders, knowing it wouldn't be safe to go back on their own. Chottu felt sorry for the tiger.

'Do they have to kill the tiger?' he asked. 'If they drive him across the river he won't come back, will he?'

'Who knows?' said Nandu. 'He has found it's easy to kill our buffaloes, and when he's hungry he'll come again. We have to live too.'

Chottu was silent. He could see no way out for the tiger.

For an hour the villagers beat the jungle, shouting, drumming, and trampling the undergrowth.

The tiger had no rest. Whenever he was able to put some distance between himself and the men, he would sink down in some shady spot to rest; but, within a few minutes, the trampling and drumming would come nearer, and with an angry snarl he would get up again and pad northwards, along the narrowing strip of jungle, towards the bridge across the river.

It was about noon when the tiger finally came into the open. The boys had a clear view of him as he moved slowly along, now in the open with the sun glinting on his glossy side, now in the shade or passing through the shorter grass. He was still out of range of Kundan Singh's gun, but there was no way in which he could retreat.

He disappeared among some bushes but soon reappeared to retrace his steps. The beaters had

done their work well. The tiger was now only about a-hundred-and-fifty yards from the place where Kundan Singh waited.

The beat had closed in, the men were now bunched together. They were making a great noise, but nothing moved.

Chottu, watching from a distance, wondered: Has he slipped through the beaters? And in his heart he hoped so.

Tins clashed, drums beat, and some of the men poked into the reeds along the river bank with their spears or bamboo sticks. Perhaps one of these thrusts found its mark, because at last the tiger was roused, and with an angry, desperate snarl he charged out of the reeds, splashing his way through an inlet of mud and water.

Kundan Singh fired and missed.

The tiger rushed forward, making straight for the only way across the river – the suspension bridge that crossed it, providing a route into the hills beyond.

The suspension bridge swayed and trembled as the big tiger lurched across it. Kundan fired again, and this time the bullet grazed the tiger's shoulder.

The tiger bounded forward, lost his footing on the unfamiliar, slippery planks of the swaying bridge, and went over the side, falling headlong into the swirling water of the river.

He rose to the surface once, but the current took him under and away, and before long he was lost to view.

5

At first the villagers were glad – they felt their buffaloes were safe. Then they began to feel that something had gone out of their lives, out of the life of the forest. The forest had been shrinking year by year, as more people had moved into the area; but as long as the tiger had been there and they had heard him roar at night, they had known there was still some distance between them and the ever-spreading towns and cities. Now that the tiger had gone, it was as though a protector had gone.

The boys lay flat on their stomachs on their little mud island, and watched the monsoon clouds gathering overhead.

'The king of the jungle is dead,' said Nandu. 'There are no more tigers.'

'There have to be tigers,' said Chottu. 'Can there be an India without tigers?'

The river had carried the tiger many miles away from his old home, from the forest he had always known, and brought him ashore on the opposite bank of the river, on a strip of warm yellow sand. Here he lay in the sun, quite still, breathing slowly.

Vultures gathered and waited at a distance, some of them perching on the branches of nearby trees. But the tiger was more drowned than hurt, and as the river water oozed out of his mouth, and the warm sun made new life throb through his body, he stirred and stretched, and his glazed eyes came into focus. Raising his head, he saw trees and tall grass.

Slowly he heaved himself off the ground and moved at a crouch to where the tall grass waved in the afternoon breeze. Would he be hunted again, and shot at? There was no smell of man. The tiger moved forward with greater confidence.

There was, however, another smell in the air, a smell that reached back to the time when he was young and fresh and full of vigour; a smell that he had almost forgotten but could never really forget – the smell of a tigress.

He lifted his head, and new life surged through his limbs. He gave a deep roar, 'A-oonh!' and moved purposefully through the tall grass. And the roar came back to him, calling him, urging him forward; a roar that meant there would be more tigers in the land!

That night, half asleep on his cot, Chottu heard the tigers roaring to each other across the river, and he recognised the roar of his own tiger. And from the vigour of its roar he knew that it was alive and safe; and he was glad.

'Let there be tigers forever,' he whispered into the darkness before he fell asleep.

Monkey Trouble

Grandfather bought Tutu from a street entertainer for the sum of ten rupees. The man had three monkeys. Tutu was the smallest, but the most mischievous. She was tied up most of the time. The little monkey looked so miserable with a collar and chain that Grandfather decided it would be much happier in our home. Grandfather had a weakness for keeping unusual pets. It was a habit that I, at the age of eight or nine, used to encourage.

Grandmother at first objected to having a monkey in the house. 'You have enough pets as it is,' she said, referring to Grandfather's goat, several white mice, and a small tortoise.

'But I don't have any,' I said.

'You're wicked enough for two monkeys. One boy in the house is all I can take.'

'Ah, but Tutu isn't a boy,' said Grandfather triumphantly. 'This is a little girl monkey!'

Grandmother gave in. She had always wanted a little girl in the house. She believed girls were less troublesome than boys. Tutu was to prove her wrong.

She was a pretty little monkey. Her bright eyes sparkled with mischief beneath deep-set eyebrows. And her teeth, which were a pearly white, were often revealed in a grin that frightened the wits out of Aunt Ruby, whose nerves had already suffered from the presence of Grandfather's pet python. But this was my grandparents' house, and aunts and uncles had to put up with our pets.

Tutu's hands had a dried-up look, as though they had been pickled in the sun for many years. One of the first things I taught her was to shake hands, and this she insisted on doing with all who visited the house. Peppery Major Malik would have to stoop and shake hands with Tutu before he could enter the drawing room, otherwise Tutu would climb onto his shoulder and stay there, roughing up his hair and playing with his moustache.

Uncle Benji couldn't stand any of our pets and took a particular dislike to Tutu, who was always making faces at him. But as Uncle Benji was never in a job for long, and depended on Grandfather's good-natured generosity, he had to shake hands with Tutu, like everyone else.

Tutu's fingers were quick and wicked. And her tail, while adding to her good looks (Grandfather believed a tail would add to anyone's good looks!), also served as a third hand. She could use it to hang from a branch, and it was capable of scooping up any delicacy that might be out of reach of her hands.

On one of Aunt Ruby's visits, loud shrieks from her bedroom brought us running to see what was wrong. It was only Tutu trying on Aunt Ruby's petticoats! They were much too large, of course, and when Aunt Ruby entered the room, all she saw was a faceless white blob jumping up and down on the bed.

We disentangled Tutu and soothed Aunt Ruby. I gave Tutu a bunch of sweet-peas to make her happy. Granny didn't like anyone plucking her sweet-peas, so I took some from Major Malik's garden while he was having his afternoon siesta.

Then Uncle Benji complained that his hairbrush was missing. We found Tutu sunning herself on the back veranda, using the hairbrush to scratch her armpits.

I took it from her and handed it back to Uncle Benji with an apology; but he flung the brush away with an oath.

'Such a fuss about nothing,' I said. 'Tutu doesn't have fleas!'

'No, and she bathes more often than Benji,' said Grandfather, who had borrowed Aunt Ruby's shampoo to give Tutu a bath.

All the same, Grandmother objected to Tutu being given the run of the house. Tutu had to spend her nights in the outhouse, in the company of the goat. They got on quite well, and it was not long before Tutu was seen sitting comfortably on the back of the goat, while the goat roamed the back garden in search of its favourite grass.

The day Grandfather had to visit Meerut to collect his railway pension, he decided to take Tutu and me along to keep us both out of mischief, he said. To prevent Tutu from wandering about on the train, causing inconvenience to passengers, she was provided with a large black travelling bag. This, with some straw at the bottom, became her compartment. Grandfather and I paid for our seats, and we took Tutu along as hand baggage.

There was enough space for Tutu to look out of the bag occasionally, and to be fed with bananas and biscuits, but she could not get her hands through the opening and the canvas was too strong for her to bite her way through.

Tutu's efforts to get out only had the effect of making the bag roll about on the floor or occasionally jump into the air – an exhibition that attracted a curious crowd of onlookers at the Dehra and Meerut railway stations.

Anyway, Tutu remained in the bag as far as Meerut, but while Grandfather was producing our tickets at the turnstile, she suddenly poked her head out of the bag and gave the ticket collector a wide grin.

The poor man was taken aback. But, with great presence of mind and much to Grandfather's annoyance, he said, 'Sir, you have a dog with you. You'll have to buy a ticket for it.'

'It's not a dog!' said Grandfather indignantly. 'This is a baby monkey of the species *macacus-mischievous*, closely related to the human species *homus-horriblis*! And there is no charge for babies!'

'It's as big as a cat,' said the ticket collector, 'Cats and dogs have to be paid for.'

'But, I tell you, it's only a baby!' protested Grandfather.

'Have you a birth certificate to prove that?' demanded the ticket collector.

'Next, you'll be asking to see her mother,' snapped Grandfather.

In vain did he take Tutu out of the bag. In vain did he try to prove that a young monkey did not qualify as a dog or a cat or even as a quadruped. Tutu was classified as a dog by the ticket collector, and five rupees were handed over as her fare.

Then Grandfather, just to get his own back, took from his pocket the small tortoise that he sometimes carried about, and said: 'And what must I pay for this, since you charge for all creatures great and small?'

The ticket collector looked closely at the tortoise, prodded it with his forefinger, gave Grandfather a triumphant look, and said, 'No charge, sir. It is not a dog!'

Winters in North India can be very cold. A great treat for Tutu on winter evenings was the large bowl of hot water given to her by Grandfather for a bath. Tutu would cunningly test the temperature with her hand, then gradually step into the bath, first one foot, then the other (as she had seen me doing) until she was in the water upto her neck.

Once comfortable, she would take the soap in her hands or feet and rub herself all over. When the water became cold, she would get out and run as quickly as she could to the kitchen fire in order to dry herself. If anyone laughed at her during this performance, Tutu's feelings would be hurt and she would refuse to go on with the bath.

One day Tutu almost succeeded in boiling herself alive. Grandmother had left a large kettle on the fire for tea. And Tutu, all by herself and with nothing better to do, decided to remove the lid. Finding the water just warm enough for a bath, she got in, with her head sticking out from the open kettle.

This was fine for a while, until the water began to get heated. Tutu raised herself a little. But finding it cold outside, she sat down again. She continued hopping up and down for some time, until Grandmother returned and hauled her, half-boiled, out of the kettle.

'What's for tea today?' asked Uncle Benji gleefully. 'Boiled eggs and a half-boiled monkey?'

But Tutu was none the worse for the adventure and continued to bathe more regularly than Uncle Benji.

Aunt Ruby was a frequent taker of baths. This met with Tutu's approval – so much so that, one day, when Aunt Ruby had finished shampooing her hair, she looked up through a lather of bubbles and soap-suds to see Tutu sitting opposite her in the bath, following her example.

One day Aunt Ruby took us all by surprise. She announced that she had become engaged. We had always thought Aunt Ruby would never marry – she had often said so herself – but it appeared that the right man had now come along in the person of Rocky Fernandes, a schoolteacher from Goa.

Rocky was a tall, firm-jawed, good-natured man, a couple of years younger than Aunt Ruby. He had a fine baritone voice and sang in the manner of the great Nelson Eddy. As Grandmother liked baritone singers, Rocky was soon in her good books.

'But what on earth does he see in her?' Uncle Benji wanted to know.

'More than any girl has seen in you!' snapped Grandmother. 'Ruby's a fine girl. And they're both teachers. Maybe they can start a school of their own.'

Rocky visited the house quite often and brought me chocolates and cashew nuts, of which he seemed to have an unlimited supply. He also taught me several marching songs. Naturally, I approved of Rocky. Aunt Ruby won my grudging admiration for having made such a wise choice.

One day I overheard them talking of going to the bazaar to buy an engagement ring. I decided I would go along, too. But as Aunt Ruby had made it clear that she did not want me around, I decided that I had better follow at a discreet distance. Tutu, becoming aware that a mission of some importance was under way, decided to follow me. But as I had not invited her along, she too decided to keep out of sight.

Once in the crowded bazaar, I was able to get quite close to Aunt Ruby and Rocky without being spotted. I waited until they had settled down in a large jewellery shop before sauntering past and spotting them, as though by accident. Aunt Ruby wasn't too pleased at seeing me, but Rocky waved and called out, 'Come and join us! Help your aunt choose a beautiful ring!'

The whole thing seemed to be a waste of good money, but I did not say so – Aunt Ruby was giving me one of her more unloving looks.

'Look, these are pretty!' I said, pointing to some cheap, bright agates set in white metal. But Aunt Ruby wasn't looking. She was immersed in a case of diamonds.

'Why not a ruby for Aunt Ruby?' I suggested, trying to please her.

'That's her lucky stone,' said Rocky. 'Diamonds are the thing for engagements.' And he started singing a song about a diamond being a girl's best friend.

While the jeweller and Aunt Ruby were sifting through the diamond rings, and Rocky was trying out another tune, Tutu had slipped into the shop without being noticed by anyone but me. A little squeal of delight was the first sign she gave of her presence. Everyone looked up to see her trying on a pretty necklace.

'And what are those stones?' I asked.

'They look like pearls,' said Rocky.

'They *are* pearls,' said the shopkeeper, making a grab for them.

'It's that dreadful monkey!' cried Aunt Ruby. 'I knew that boy would bring him here!'

The necklace was already adorning Tutu's neck. I thought she looked rather nice in pearls, but she gave us no time to admire the effect. Springing out of our reach, Tutu dodged around Rocky, slipped between my legs, and made for the crowded road. I ran after her, shouting to her to stop, but she wasn't listening.

There were no branches to assist Tutu in her progress, but she used the heads and shoulders of people as springboards and so made rapid headway through the bazaar.

The jeweller left his shop and ran after us. So did Rocky. So did several bystanders, who had seen the incident. And others, who had no idea what it was all about, joined in the chase. As Grandfather used to say, 'In a crowd, everyone plays follow-the-leader, even when they don't know who's leading.' Not everyone knew that the leader was Tutu. Only the front runners could see her.

She tried to make her escape speedier by leaping onto the back of a passing scooterist. The scooter swerved into a fruit stall and came to a standstill under a heap of bananas, while the scooterist found himself in the arms of an indignant fruitseller. Tutu peeled a banana and ate part of it, before deciding to move on.

From an awning she made an emergency landing on a washerman's donkey. The donkey promptly panicked and rushed down the road, while bundles of washing fell by the wayside. The washerman joined in the chase. Children on their way to school decided that there was something better to do than attend classes. With shouts of glee, they soon overtook their panting elders.

Tutu finally left the bazaar and took a road leading in the direction of our house. But knowing that she would be caught and locked up once she got home, she decided to end the chase by ridding herself of the necklace. Deftly removing it from her neck, she flung it in the small canal that ran down the road.

The jeweller, with a cry of anguish, plunged into the canal. So did Rocky. So did I. So did several other people, both adults and children. It was to be a treasure hunt!

Some twenty minutes later, Rocky shouted, 'I've found it!' Covered in mud, water-lilies, ferns and tadpoles, we emerged from the canal, and Rocky presented the necklace to the relieved shopkeeper.

Everyone trudged back to the bazaar to find Aunt Ruby waiting in the shop, still trying to make up her mind about a suitable engagement ring.

Finally the ring was bought, the engagement was announced, and a date was set for the wedding.

'I don't want that monkey anywhere near us on our wedding day,' declared Aunt Ruby.

'We'll lock her up in the outhouse,' promised Grandfather. 'And we'll let her out only after you've left for your honeymoon.'

A few days before the wedding I found Tutu in the kitchen, helping Grandmother prepare the wedding cake. Tutu often helped with the cooking and, when Grandmother wasn't looking, added herbs, spices, and other interesting items to the pots – so that occasionally we found a chilli in the custard or an onion in the jelly or a strawberry floating in the chicken soup.

Sometimes these additions improved a dish, sometimes they did not. Uncle Benji lost a tooth when he bit firmly into a sandwich which contained walnut shells.

I'm not sure exactly what went into that wedding cake when Grandmother wasn't looking – she insisted that Tutu was always very well-behaved in the kitchen – but I did spot Tutu stirring in some red chilli sauce, bitter gourd seeds, and a generous helping of egg-shells!

It's true that some of the guests were not seen for several days after the wedding, but no one said anything against the cake. Most people thought it had an interesting flavour.

The great day dawned, and the wedding guests made their way to the little church that stood on the outskirts of Dehra – a town with a church, two mosques, and several temples.

I had offered to dress Tutu up as a bridesmaid and bring her along, but no one except Grandfather thought it was a good idea. So I was an obedient boy and locked Tutu in the outhouse. I did, however, leave the skylight open a little. Grandmother had always said that fresh air was good for growing children, and I thought Tutu should have her share of it.

The wedding ceremony went without a hitch. Aunt Ruby looked a picture, and Rocky looked like a film star.

Grandfather played the organ, and did so with such gusto that the small choir could hardly be heard. Grandmother cried a little. I sat quietly in a corner, with the little tortoise on my lap.

When the service was over, we trooped out into the sunshine and made our way back to the house for the reception.

The feast had been laid out on tables in the garden. As the gardener had been left in charge, everything was in order. Tutu was on her best behaviour. She had, it appeared, used the skylight to avail of more fresh air outside, and now sat beside the three-tier wedding cake, guarding it against crows, squirrels and the goat. She greeted the guests with squeals of delight.

It was too much for Aunt Ruby. She flew at Tutu in a rage. And Tutu, sensing that she was not welcome, leapt away, taking with her the top tier of the wedding cake.

Led by Major Malik, we followed her into the orchard, only to find that she had climbed to the top of the jackfruit tree. From there she proceeded to pelt us with bits of wedding cake. She had also managed to get hold of a bag of confetti, and when she ran out of cake she showered us with confetti.

'That's more like it!' said the good-humoured Rocky. 'Now let's return to the party, folks!'

Uncle Benji remained with Major Malik, determined to chase Tutu away. He kept throwing stones into the tree, until he received a large piece of cake bang on his nose. Muttering threats, he returned to the party, leaving the major to do battle.

When the festivities were finally over, Uncle Benji took the old car out of the garage and drove up the veranda steps. He was going to drive Aunt Ruby and Rocky to the nearby hill resort of Mussoorie, where they would have their honeymoon.

Watched by family and friends, Aunt Ruby climbed into the back seat. She waved regally to everyone. She leant out of the window and offered me her cheek and I had to kiss her farewell. Everyone wished them luck.

As Rocky burst into song, Uncle Benji opened the throttle and stepped on the accelerator. The car shot forward in a cloud of dust.

Rocky and Aunt Ruby continued to wave to us. And so did Tutu, from her perch on the rear bumper! She was clutching a bag in her hands and showering confetti on all who stood in the driveway.

'They don't know Tutu's with them!' I exclaimed. 'She'll go all the way to Mussoorie! Will Aunt Ruby let her stay with them?'

'Tutu might ruin the honeymoon,' said Grandfather. 'But don't worry – our Benji will bring her back!'

Snake Trouble

1

After retiring from the Indian Railways and settling in Dehra, Grandfather often made his days (and ours) more exciting by keeping unusual pets. He paid a snake-charmer in the bazaar twenty rupees for a young python. Then, to the delight of a curious group of boys and girls, he slung the python over his shoulder and brought it home.

I was with him at the time, and felt very proud walking beside Grandfather. He was popular in Dehra, especially among the poorer people, and everyone greeted him politely without seeming to notice the python. They were, in fact, quite used to seeing him in the company of strange creatures.

The first to see us arrive was Tutu the monkey, who was swinging from a branch of the jackfruit tree. One look at the python, ancient enemy of his race, and he fled into the house squealing with fright. Then our parrot, Popeye, who had his perch on the veranda, set up the most awful shrieking and whistling. His whistle was like that of a steam-engine. He had learnt to do this in earlier days, when we had lived near railway stations.

The noise brought Grandmother to the veranda, where she nearly fainted at the sight of the python curled round Grandfather's neck.

Grandmother put up with most of his pets, but she drew the line at reptiles. Even a sweet-tempered lizard made her blood run cold. There was little chance that she would allow a python in the house.

'It will strangle you to death!' she cried.

'Nonsense,' said Grandfather. 'He's only a young fellow.'

'He'll soon get used to us,' I added, by way of support.

'He might, indeed,' said Grandmother, 'but I have no intention of getting used to him. And your Aunt Ruby is coming to stay with us tomorrow. She'll leave the minute she knows there's a snake in the house.'

'Well, perhaps we should show it to her first thing,' said Grandfather, who found Aunt Ruby rather tiresome.

'Get rid of it right away,' said Grandmother.

'I can't let it loose in the garden. It might find its way into the chicken shed, and then where will we be?'

'Minus a few chickens,' I said reasonably, but this only made Grandmother more determined to get rid of the python.

'Lock that awful thing in the bathroom,' she said. 'Go and find the man you bought it from, and get him to come here and collect it! He can keep the money you gave him.'

Grandfather and I took the snake into the bathroom and placed it in an empty tub. Looking a bit crestfallen, he said, 'Perhaps your grandmother is right. I'm not worried about Aunt Ruby, but we don't want the python to get hold of Tutu or Popeye.'

We hurried off to the bazaar in search of the snake-charmer but hadn't gone far when we found several snake-charmers looking for us. They had heard that Grandfather was buying snakes, and they had brought with them snakes of various sizes and descriptions.

'No, no!' protested Grandfather. 'We don't want more snakes. We want to return the one we bought.'

But the man who had sold it to us had, apparently, returned to his village in the jungle, looking for another python for Grandfather; and the other snake-charmers were not interested in buying, only in selling. In order to shake them off, we had to return home by a roundabout route, climbing a wall and cutting through an orchard. We found Grandmother pacing up and down the veranda. One look at our faces and she knew we had failed to get rid of the snake.

'All right,' said Grandmother. 'Just take it away yourselves and see that it doesn't come back.'

'We'll get rid of it, Grandmother,' I said confidently. 'Don't you worry.'

Grandfather opened the bathroom door and stepped into the room. I was close behind him. We couldn't see the python anywhere.

'He's gone,' announced Grandfather.

'We left the window open,' I said.

'Deliberately, no doubt,' said Grandmother. 'But it couldn't have gone far. You'll have to search the grounds.'

A careful search was made of the house, the roof, the kitchen, the garden and the chicken shed, but there was no sign of the python.

'He must have gone over the garden wall,' Grandfather said cheerfully. 'He'll be well away by now!'

The python did not reappear, and when Aunt Ruby arrived with enough luggage to show that she had come for a long visit, there was only the parrot to greet her with a series of long, ear-splitting whistles.

2

For a couple of days Grandfather and I were a little worried that the python might make a sudden reappearance, but when he didn't show up again we felt he had gone for good. Aunt Ruby had to put up with Tutu the monkey making faces at her, something I did only when she wasn't looking; and she complained that Popeye shrieked loudest when she was in the room; but she was used to them, and knew she would have to bear with them if she was going to stay with us.

And then, one evening, we were startled by a scream from the garden.

Seconds later Aunt Ruby came flying up the veranda steps, gasping, 'In the guava tree! I was reaching for a guava when I saw it staring at me. The look in its eyes! As though it would eat me alive –'

'Calm down, dear,' urged Grandmother, sprinkling rose water over my aunt. 'Tell us, what *did* you see?'

'A snake!' sobbed Aunt Ruby. 'A great boa constrictor in the guava tree. Its eyes were terrible, and it looked at me in such a queer way.'

'Trying to tempt you with a guava, no doubt,' said Grandfather, turning away to hide his smile. He gave me a look full of meaning, and I hurried out into the garden. But when I got to the guava tree, the python (if it had been the python) had gone.

'Aunt Ruby must have frightened it off,' I told Grandfather.

'I'm not surprised,' he said. 'But it will be back, Ranji. I think it has taken a fancy to your aunt.'

Sure enough, the python began to make brief but frequent appearances, usually up in the most unexpected places.

One morning I found him curled up on a dressing-table, gazing at his own reflection in the mirror. I went for Grandfather, but by the time we returned the python had moved on.

He was seen again in the garden, and one day I spotted him climbing the iron ladder to the roof. I set off after him, and was soon up the ladder, which I had climbed up many times. I arrived on the flat roof just in time to see the snake disappearing down a drainpipe. The end of his tail was visible for a few moments and then that too disappeared.

'I think he lives in the drainpipe,' I told Grandfather.

'Where does it get its food?' asked Grandmother.

'Probably lives on those field rats that used to be such a nuisance. Remember, they lived in the drainpipes, too.'

'Hmm...' Grandmother looked thoughtful. 'A snake has its uses. Well, as long as it keeps to the roof and prefers rats to chickens...'

But the python did not confine itself to the roof. Piercing shrieks from Aunt Ruby had us all rushing to her room. There was the python on *her* dressing-table, apparently admiring himself in the mirror.

'All the attention he's been getting has probably made him conceited,' said Grandfather, picking up the python to the accompaniment of further shrieks from Aunt Ruby. 'Would you like to hold him for a minute, Ruby? He seems to have taken a fancy to you.'

Aunt Ruby ran from the room and onto the veranda, where she was greeted with whistles of derision from Popeye the parrot. Poor Aunt Ruby! She cut short her stay by a week and returned to Lucknow, where she was a schoolteacher. She said she felt safer in her school than she did in our house.

3

Having seen Grandfather handle the python with such ease and confidence, I decided I would do likewise. So the next time I saw the snake climbing the ladder to the roof, I climbed up alongside him. He stopped, and I stopped too. I put out my hand, and he slid over my arm and up to my shoulder. As I did not want him coiling round my neck, I gripped him with both hands and carried him down to the garden. He didn't seem to mind.

The snake felt rather cold and slippery and at first he gave me goose pimples. But I soon got used to him, and he must have liked the way I handled him, because when I set him down he wanted to climb up my leg. As I had other things to do, I dropped him in a large empty basket that had been left out in the garden. He stared out at me with unblinking, expressionless eyes. There was no way of knowing what he was thinking, if indeed he thought at all.

I went off for a bicycle ride, and when I returned, I found Grandmother picking guavas and dropping them into the basket. The python must have gone elsewhere.

When the basket was full, Grandmother said, 'Will you take these over to Major Malik?' It's his birthday and I want to give him a nice surprise.'

I fixed the basket on the carrier of my cycle and pedalled off to Major Malik's house at the end of the road. The major met me on the steps of his house.

'And what has your kind granny sent me today, Ranji?' he asked.

'A surprise for your birthday, sir,' I said, and put the basket down in front of him.

The python, who had been buried beneath all the guavas, chose this moment to wake up and stand straight up to a height of several feet. Guavas tumbled all over the place. The major uttered an oath and dashed indoors.

I pushed the python back into the basket, picked it up, mounted the bicycle, and rode out of the gate in record time. And it was as well that I did so, because Major Malik came charging out of the house armed with a double-barrelled shotgun, which he was waving all over the place.

'Did you deliver the guavas?' asked Grandmother when I got back.

'I delivered them,' I said truthfully.

'And was he pleased?'

'He's going to write and thank you,' I said.

And he did.

'*Thank you for the lovely surprise*,' he wrote, '*Obviously you could not have known that my doctor had advised me against any undue excitement. My blood-pressure has been rather high. The sight of your grandson does not improve it. All the same, it's the thought that matters and I take it all in good humour...'*

'What a strange letter,' said Grandmother. 'He must be ill, poor man. Are guavas bad for blood pressure?'

'Not by themselves, they aren't,' said Grandfather, who had an inkling of what had happened. 'But together with other things they can be a bit upsetting.'

4

Just when all of us, including Grandmother, were getting used to having the python about the house and grounds, it was decided that we would be going to Lucknow for a few months.

Lucknow was a large city, about three hundred miles from Dehra. Aunt Ruby lived and worked there. We would be staying with her, and so of course we couldn't take any pythons, monkeys or other unusual pets with us.

'What about Popeye?' I asked.

'Popeye isn't a pet,' said Grandmother. 'He's one of us. He comes too.'

And so the Dehra railway platform was thrown into confusion by the shrieks and whistles of our parrot, who could imitate both the guard's whistle and the whistle of a train. People dashed into their compartments, thinking the train was about to leave, only to realise that the guard hadn't blown his whistle after all. When they got down, Popeye would let out another shrill whistle, which sent everyone rushing for the train again. This happened several times until the guard actually blew his whistle. Then nobody bothered to get on, and several passengers were left behind.

'Can't you gag that parrot?' asked Grandfather, as the train moved out of the station and picked up speed.

'I'll do nothing of the sort,' said Grandmother. 'I've bought a ticket for him, and he's entitled to enjoy the journey as much as anyone.'

Whenever we stopped at a station, Popeye objected to fruit-sellers and other people poking their heads in through the windows. Before the journey was over, he had nipped two fingers and a nose, and tweaked a ticket-inspector's ear.

It was to be a night journey, and presently Grandmother covered herself with a blanket and stretched out on the berth. 'It's been a tiring day. I think I'll go to sleep,' she said.

'Aren't we going to eat anything?' I asked.

'I'm not hungry – I had something before we left the house. You two help yourselves from the picnic hamper.'

Grandmother dozed off, and even Popeye started nodding, lulled to sleep by the clackety-clack of the wheels and the steady puffing of the steam-engine.

'Well, I'm hungry,' I said. 'What did Granny make for us?'

'Stuffed samosas, omelettes, and tandoori chicken. It's all in the hamper under the berth.

I tugged at the cane box and dragged it into the middle of the compartment. The straps were loosely tied. No sooner had I undone them than the lid flew open, and I let out a gasp of surprise.

In the hamper was a python, curled up contentedly. There was no sign of our dinner.

'It's a python,' I said. 'And it's finished all our dinner.'

'Nonsense,' said Grandfather, joining me near the hamper. 'Pythons won't eat omelette and samosas. They like their food alive! Why, this isn't our hamper. The one with our food in it must have been left behind! Wasn't it Major Malik who helped us with our luggage? I think he's got his own back on us by changing the hamper!'

Grandfather snapped the hamper shut and pushed it back beneath the berth.

'Don't let Grandmother see him,' he said. 'She might think we brought him along on purpose.'

'Well, I'm hungry,' I complained.

'Wait till we get to the next station, then we can buy some pakoras. Meanwhile, try some of Popeye's green chillies.'

'No thanks,' I said. 'You have them, Grandad.'

And Grandfather, who could eat chillies plain, popped a couple into his mouth and munched away contentedly.

✧

A little after midnight there was a great clamour at the end of the corridor. Popeye made complaining squawks, and Grandfather and I got up to see what was wrong.

Suddenly there were cries of 'Snake, snake!'

I looked under the berth. The hamper was open.

'The python's out,' I said, and Grandfather dashed out of the compartment in his pyjamas. I was close behind.

About a dozen passengers were bunched together outside the washroom.

'Anything wrong?' asked Grandfather casually.

'We can't get into the toilet,' said someone. 'There's a huge snake inside.'

'Let me take a look,' said Grandfather. 'I know all about snakes.'

The passengers made way, and Grandfather and I entered the washroom together, but there was no sign of the python.

'He must have got out through the ventilator,' said Grandfather. 'By now he'll be in another compartment!'

Emerging from the washroom, he told the assembled passengers 'It's gone! Nothing to worry about. Just a harmless young python.'

When we got back to our compartment, Grandmother was sitting up on her berth.

'I *knew* you'd do something foolish behind my back,' she scolded. 'You told me you'd left that creature behind, and all the time it was with us on the train.'

Grandfather tried to explain that we had nothing to do with it, that this python had been smuggled onto the train by Major Malik, but Grandmother was unconvinced.

'Anyway, it's gone,' said Grandfather. 'It must have fallen out of the washroom window. We're over a hundred miles from Dehra, so you'll never see it again.'

Even as he spoke, the train slowed down and lurched to a grinding halt.

'No station here,' said Grandfather, putting his head out of the window.

Someone came rushing along the embankment, waving his arms and shouting.

'I do believe it's the stoker,' said Grandfather. 'I'd better go and see what's wrong.'

'I'm coming too,' I said, and together we hurried along the length of the stationary train until we reached the engine.

'What's up?' called Grandfather. 'Anything I can do to help? I know all about engines.'

But the engine-driver was speechless. And who could blame him? The python had curled itself about his legs, and the driver was too petrified to move.

'Just leave it to us,' said Grandfather, and, dragging the python off the driver, he dumped the snake in my arms. The engine-driver sank down on the floor, pale and trembling.

'I think I'd better driver the engine,' said Grandfather. 'We don't want to be late getting into Lucknow. Your aunt will be expecting us!' And before the astonished driver could protest, Grandfather had released the brakes and set the engine in motion.

'We've left the stoker behind,' I said.

'Never mind. You can shovel the coal.'

Only too glad to help Grandfather drive an engine, I dropped the python in the driver's lap and started shovelling coal. The engine picked up speed and we were soon rushing through the darkness, sparks flying skywards and the steam-whistle shrieking almost with pause.

'You're going too fast!' cried the driver.

'Making up for lost time,' said Grandfather. 'Why did the stoker run away?'

'He went for the guard. You've left them both behind!'

5

Early next morning the train steamed safely into Lucknow. Explanations were in order, but as the Lucknow station-master was an old friend of Grandfather, all was well. We had arrived twenty minutes early, and while Grandfather went off to have a cup of tea with the engine-driver and the station-master, I returned the python to the hamper and helped Grandmother with the luggage. Popeye stayed perched on Grandmother's shoulder, eyeing the busy platform with deep distrust. He was the first to see Aunt Ruby striding down the platform, and let out a warning whistle.

Aunt Ruby, a lover of good food, immediately spotted the picnic hamper, picked it up and said, 'It's quite heavy. You must have kept something for me! I'll carry it out to the taxi.'

'We hardly ate anything,' I said.

'It seems ages since I tasted something cooked by your granny.' And after that there was no getting the hamper away from Aunt Ruby.

Glancing at it, I thought I saw the lid bulging, but I had tied it down quite firmly this time and there was little likelihood of its suddenly bursting open.

Grandfather joined us outside the station and we were soon settled inside the taxi. Aunt Ruby gave instructions to the driver and we shot off in a cloud of dust.

'I'm dying to see what's in the hamper,' said Aunt Ruby. 'Can't I take just a little peek?'

'Not now,' said Grandfather. 'First let's enjoy the breakfast you've got waiting for us.'

Popeye, perched proudly on Grandmother's shoulder, kept one suspicious eye on the quivering hamper.

When we got to Aunt Ruby's house, we found breakfast laid out on the dining-table.

'It isn't much,' said Aunt Ruby. 'But we'll supplement it with what you've brought in the hamper.'

Placing the hamper on the table, she lifted the lid and peered inside. And promptly fainted.

Grandfather picked up the python, took it into the garden, and draped it over a branch of a pomegranate tree.

When Aunt Ruby recovered, she insisted that she had seen a huge snake in the picnic hamper. We showed her the empty basket.

'You're seeing things,' said Grandfather. 'You've been working too hard.'

'Teaching is a very tiring job,' I said solemnly.

Grandmother said nothing. But Popeye broke into loud squawks and whistles, and soon everyone, including a slightly hysterical Aunt Ruby, was doubled up with laughter.

But the snake must have tired of the joke because we never saw it again!

Those Three Bears

Most Himalayan villages lie in the valleys, where there are small streams, some farmland, and protection from the biting winds that come through the mountain passes in winter. The houses are usually made of large stones and have sloping slate roofs so the heavy monsoon rain can run off easily. During the sunny autumn months, the roofs are often covered with pumpkins, left there to ripen in the sun.

One October night, when I was sleeping at a friend's house in a village in these hills, I was awakened by a rumbling and thumping on the roof. I woke my friend and asked him what was happening.

'It's only a bear,' he said.

'Is it trying to get in?'

'No. It's after the pumpkins.'

A little later, when we looked out of a window, we saw a black bear making off through a field, leaving a trail of half-eaten pumpkins.

In winter, when snow covers the higher ranges, the Himalayan bears come to lower altitudes in search of food. Sometimes they forage in fields and because they are shortsighted and suspicious of anything that moves, they can be dangerous. But, like most wild animals, they avoid humans as much as possible.

Village folk always advice me to run downhill if chased by a bear. They say bears find it easier to run uphill than down. I am yet to be chased by a bear, and will happily skip the experience. But I have seen a few of these mountain bears in India, and they are always fascinating to watch.

Himalayan bears enjoy pumpkins, corn, plums, and apricots. Once, while I was sitting in an oak tree hoping to see a pair of pine martens that lived nearby, I heard the whining grumble of a bear, and presently a small bear ambled into the clearing beneath the tree.

He was little more than a cub, and I was not alarmed. I sat very still, waiting to see what he would do.

He put his nose to the ground and sniffed his way along until he came to a large anthill. Here he began huffing and puffing, blowing rapidly in and out of his nostrils, so that the dust from the anthill flew in all directions. But the anthill had been deserted, and so, grumbling, the bear made his way up a nearby plum tree. Soon he was perched high in the branches. It was then that he saw me.

The bear at once scrambled several feet higher up the tree and lay flat on a branch. Since it wasn't a very big branch, there was a lot of bear showing on either side. He tucked his head behind another branch. He could no longer see me, so he apparently was satisfied that he was hidden, although he couldn't help grumbling.

Like all bears, this one was full of curiosity. So, slowly, inch by inch, his black snout appeared over the edge of the branch. As soon as he saw me, he drew his head back and hid his face.

He did this several times. I waited until he wasn't looking, then moved some way down my tree. When the bear looked over and saw that I was missing, he was so pleased that he stretched right across to another branch and helped himself to a plum. I couldn't help bursting into laughter.

The startled young bear tumbled out of the tree, dropped through the branches some fifteen feet, and landed with a thump in a pile of dried leaves. He was unhurt, but fled from the clearing, grunting and squealing all the way.

Another time, my friend Prem told me, a bear had been active in his cornfield. We took up a post at night in an old cattle shed, which gave a clear view of the moonlit field.

A little after midnight, a female bear came down to the edge of the field. She seemed to sense that we had been about. She was hungry, however. So, after standing on her hind legs and peering around to make sure the field was empty, she came cautiously out of the forest.

Her attention was soon distracted by some Tibetan prayer flags, which had been strung between two trees. She gave a grunt of disapproval and began to back away, but the fluttering of the flags was a puzzle that she wanted to solve. So she stopped and watched them.

Soon the bear advanced to within a few feet of the flags, examining them from various angles. Then, seeing that they posed no danger, she went right up to the flags and pulled them down. Grunting with apparent satisfaction, she moved into the field of corn.

Prem had decided that he didn't want to lose any more of his crop, so he started shouting. His children woke up and soon came running from the house, banging on empty kerosene tins.

Deprived of her dinner, the bear made off in a bad temper. She ran downhill at a good speed, and I was glad that I was not in her way.

Uphill or downhill, an angry bear is best given a very wide path.

The Coral Tree

The night had been hot, the rain frequent, and I had been sleeping on the verandah instead of in the house. I was in my twenties, had begun to earn a living and felt I had certain responsibilities.

In a short time, a *tonga* would take me to the railway station, and from there a train would take me to Bombay, and then a ship would take me to England. There would be work, interviews, a job, a different kind of life, so many things that this small bungalow of my grandfather would be remembered fitfully, in rare moments of reflection.

When I awoke on the veranda, I saw a grey morning, smelt the rain on the red earth and remembered that I had to go away. A girl was standing on the veranda porch, looking at me very seriously. When I saw her, I sat up in bed with a start.

She was a small dark girl, her eyes big and black, her pigtails tied up in a bright red ribbon, and she was fresh and clean like the rain and the red earth.

She stood looking at me and was very serious.

'Hullo,' I said, smiling and trying to put her at ease. But the girl was business-like and acknowledged my greeting with a brief nod.

'Can I do anything for you?' I asked, stretching my limbs. 'Do you stay nearby?'

With great assurance she said, 'Yes, but I can stay on my own.'

'You're like me,' I said, and for a while, forgot about being an old man of twenty. 'I like to be on my own but I'm going away today.'

'Oh,' she said, a little breathlessly.

'Would you care to go to England?'

'I want to go everywhere,' she said. 'To America and Africa and Japan and Honolulu.'

'Maybe you will,' I said. 'I'm going everywhere, and no one can stop me... But what is it you want, what did you come for?'

'I want some flowers but I can't reach them.' She waved her hand towards the garden, 'That tree, see?'

The coral tree stood in front of the house surrounded by pools of water and broken, fallen blossoms. The branches of the tree were thick with scarlet, pea-shaped flowers.

'All right, just let me get ready.'

The tree was easy to climb and I made myself comfortable on one of the lower branches, smiling down at the serious upturned face of the girl.

'I'll throw them down to you,' I said.

I bent a branch but the wood was young and green and I had to twist it several times before it snapped.

'I'm not sure I ought to do this,' I said as I dropped the flowering branch to the girl.

'Don't worry,' she said.

I felt a sudden nostalgic longing for childhood and an urge to remain behind in my grandfather's house with its tangled memories and ghosts of yesteryear. But I was the only one left and what could I do except climb tamarind and jackfruit trees?

'Have you many friends?' I asked.

'Oh yes.'

'And who is the best?'

'The cook. He lets me stay in the kitchen which is more interesting than the house. And I like to watch him cooking. And he gives me things to eat and tells me stories...'

'And who is your second best friend?'

She inclined her head to one side and thought very hard.

'I'll make you second best,' she said.

I sprinkled coral blossoms on her head. 'That's very kind of you. I'm happy to be second best.'

A *tonga* bell sounded at the gate and I looked out from the tree and said, 'It's come for me. I have to go now.'

I climbed down.

'Will you help me with my suitcases?' I asked, as we walked together towards the veranda. 'There's no one here to help me. I am the last to go. Not because I want to go but because I have to.'

I sat down on the cot and packed a few last things in my suitcase. All the doors of the house were locked. On my way to the station, I would leave the keys with the caretaker. I had already given instructions to the agent to try and sell the house. There was nothing more to be done. We walked in silence to the waiting *tonga*, thinking and wondering about each other. The girl stood at the side of the path, on the damp earth, looking at me.

'Thank you,' I said, 'I hope I shall see you again.'

'I'll see you in London,' she said. 'Or America or Japan, I want to go everywhere.'

'I'm sure you will,' I said. 'And perhaps, I'll come back and we'll meet again in this garden. That would be nice, wouldn't it?'

She nodded and smiled. We knew it was an important moment. The *tonga* driver spoke to his pony and the carriage set off down the gravel path, rattling a little. The girl and I waved to each other. In the girl's hand was a spring of coral blossom. As she waved, the blossoms fell apart and danced lightly in the breeze.

'Goodbye!' I called.

'Goodbye!' called the girl.

The ribbon had come loose from her pigtail and lay on the ground with the coral blossoms.

And she was fresh and clean like the rain and the red earth.

The Thief's Story

I was still a thief when I met Romi. And though I was only fifteen years old, I was an experienced and fairly successful hand. Romi was watching a wrestling match when I approached him. He was about twenty-five and he looked easygoing, kind, and simple enough for my purpose. I was sure I would be able to win the young man's confidence.

'You look a bit of a wrestler yourself,' I said. There's nothing like flattery to break the ice!

'So do you,' he replied, which put me off for a moment because at that time I was rather thin and bony.

'Well,' I said modestly, 'I do wrestle a bit.'

'What's your name?'

'Hari Singh,' I lied. I took a new name every month, which kept me ahead of the police and former employers.

After these formalities Romi confined himself to commenting on the wrestlers, who were grunting, gasping, and heaving each other about. When he walked away, I followed him casually.

'Hello again,' he said.

I gave him my most appealing smile. 'I want to work for you,' I said.

'But I can't pay you anything – not for some time, anyway.'

I thought that over for a minute. Perhaps I had misjudged my man. 'Can you feed me?' I asked.

'Can you cook?'

'I can cook,' I lied again.

'If you can cook, then maybe I can feed you.'

He took me to his room over the Delhi Sweet Shop and told me I could sleep on the balcony. But the meal I cooked that night must have been terrible because Romi gave it to a stray dog and told me to be off.

But I just hung around, smiling in my most appealing way, and he couldn't help laughing.

Later, he said never mind, he'd teach me to cook. He also taught me to write my name and said he would soon teach me to write whole sentences and to add figures. I was grateful. I knew that once I could write like an educated person, there would be no limit to what I could achieve.

It was quite pleasant working for Romi. I made tea in the morning and then took my time buying the day's supplies, usually making a profit of two or three rupees. I think he knew I made a little money this way, but he didn't seem to mind.

Romi made money by fits and starts. He would borrow one week, lend the next. He kept worrying about his next cheque, but as soon as it arrived he would go out and celebrate. He wrote for the *Delhi* and *Bombay* magazines: a strange way to make a living.

One evening he came home with a small bundle of notes, saying he had just sold a book to a publisher. That night I saw him put the money in an envelope and tuck it under the mattress.

I had been working for Romi for almost a month and, apart from cheating on the shopping, had not done anything big in my real line of work. I had every opportunity for doing so. I could come and go as I pleased, and Romi was the most trusting person I had ever met.

That was why it was so difficult to rob him. It was easy for me to rob a greedy man. But robbing a nice man could be a problem. And if he doesn't notice he's being robbed, then all the spice goes out of the undertaking!

Well, it's time I got down to some real work, I told myself. If I don't take the money, he'll only waste it on his so-called friends. After all, he doesn't even give me a salary.

Romi was sleeping peacefully. A beam of moonlight reached over the balcony and fell on his bed. I sat on the floor, considering the situation. If I took the money, I could catch the 10:30 express to Lucknow. Slipping out of my blanket, I crept over to the bed.

My hand slid under the mattress, searching for the notes. When I found the packet, I drew it out without a sound. Romi sighed in his sleep and turned on his side. Startled, I moved quickly out of the room.

Once on the road, I began to run. I had the money stuffed into a vest pocket under my shirt. When I'd gotten some distance from Romi's place, I slowed to a walk and, taking the envelope from my pocket, counted the money. Seven hundred rupees in fifties. I could live like a prince for a week or two!

When I reached the station, I did not stop at the ticket office (I had never bought a ticket in my life) but dashed straight onto the platform. The Lucknow Express was just moving out. The train had still to pick up speed and I should have been able to jump into one of the compartments, but I hesitated – for some reason I can't explain – and I lost the chance to get away.

When the train had gone, I found myself standing alone on the deserted platform. I had no idea where to spend the night. I had no friends, believing that friends were more trouble than help. And I did not want to arouse curiosity by staying at one of the small hotels nearby. The only person I knew really well was the man I had robbed. Leaving the station, I walked slowly through the bazaar.

In my short career, I had made a study of people's faces after they had discovered the loss of their valuables. The greedy showed panic; the rich showed anger; the poor, resignation. But I knew that Romi's face when he discovered the theft would show only a touch of sadness – not for the loss of money, but for the loss of trust.

The night was chilly – November nights can be cold in northern India – and a shower of rain added to my discomfort. I sat down in the shelter of the clock tower. A few beggars and vagrants lay beside me, rolled up tight in their blankets. The clock showed midnight. I felt for the notes; they were soaked through.

Romi's money. In the morning, he would probably have given me five rupees to go to the movies, but now I had it all: no more cooking meals, running to the bazaar, or learning to write sentences.

Sentences! I had forgotten about them in the excitement of the theft. Writing complete sentences, I knew, could one day bring me more than a few hundred rupees. It was a simple matter to steal. But to be a really big man, a clever and respected man, was something else. I should go back to Romi, I told myself, if only to learn to read and write.

I hurried back to the room feeling very nervous, for it is much easier to steal something than to return it undetected.

I opened the door quietly, then stood in the doorway in clouded moonlight. Romi was still asleep. I crept to the head of the bed, and my hand came up with the packet of notes. I felt his breath on my hand. I remained still for a few moments. Then my fingers found the edge of the mattress, and I slipped the money beneath it.

I awoke late the next morning to find that Romi had already made the tea. He stretched out a hand to me. There was a fifty-rupee note between his fingers. My heart sank.

'I made some money yesterday,' he said. 'Now I'll be able to pay you regularly.'

My spirits rose. But when I took the note, I noticed that it was still wet from the night's rain.

So he knew what I'd done. But neither his lips nor his eyes revealed anything.

'Today we'll start writing sentences,' he said.

I smiled at Romi in my most appealing way. And the smile came by itself, without any effort.

When the Trees Walked

One morning while I was sitting beside Grandfather on the veranda steps, I noticed the tendril of a creeping vine trailing nearby. As we sat there in the soft sunshine of a North Indian winter, I saw the tendril moving slowly towards Grandfather. Twenty minutes later, it had crossed the step and was touching his feet.

There is probably a scientific explanation for the plant's behaviour – something to do with light and warmth perhaps – but I liked to think it moved across the steps simply because it wanted to be near Grandfather. One always felt like drawing close to him. Sometimes when I sat by myself beneath a tree, I would feel rather lonely but as soon as Grandfather joined me, the garden became a happy place. Grandfather had served many years in the Indian Forest Service and it was natural that he should know trees and like them. On his retirement, he built a bungalow on the outskirts of Dehradun, planting trees all around. Lime, mango, orange and guava, also eucalyptus, jacaranda, and Persian lilacs. In the fertile Doon Valley, plants and trees grew tall and strong.

There were other trees in the compound before the house was built, including an old peepul that had forced its way through the walls of an abandoned outhouse, knocking the bricks down with its vigorous growth. Peepul trees are great show offs. Even when there is no breeze, their broad-chested, slim-waisted leaves will spin like tops determined to attract your attention and invite you into the shade. Grandmother had wanted the peepul tree cut down but Grandfather had said, 'Let it be, we can always build another outhouse.'

Grandmother didn't mind trees, but she preferred growing flowers and was constantly ordering catalogues and seeds. Grandfather helped her out with the gardening not because he was crazy about flower gardens but because he liked watching butterflies and 'there's only one way to attract butterflies,' he said, 'and that is to grow flowers for them.'

Grandfather wasn't content with growing trees in our compound. During the rains, he would walk into the jungle beyond the river-bed armed with cuttings and saplings which he would plant in the forest.

'But no one ever comes here!' I had protested, the first time we did this. 'Who's going to see them?'

'See, we're not planting them simply to improve the view,' replied Grandfather. 'We're planting them for the forest and for the animals and birds who live here and need more food and shelter.'

'Of course, men need trees too,' he added. 'To keep the desert away, to attract rain, to prevent the banks of rivers from being washed away, for fruit and flowers, leaf and seed. Yes, for timber too. But men are cutting down trees without replacing them and if we don't plant a few trees ourselves, a time will come when the world will be one great desert.'

The thought of a world without trees became a sort of nightmare to me and I helped Grandfather in his tree-planting with greater enthusiasm. And while we went about our work, he taught me a poem by George Morris:

Woodman, spare that tree!
Touch not a single bough!
In youth it sheltered me,
And I'll protect it now.

'One day the trees will move again,' said Grandfather. 'They've been standing still for thousands of years but there was a time when they could walk about like people. Then along came an interfering busybody who cast a spell over them, rooting them to one place. But they're always trying to move. See how they reach out with their arms! And some of them, like the banyan tree with its travelling aerial roots, manage to get quite far.'

We found an island, a small rocky island in a dry river-bed. It was one of those river-beds so common in the foothills, which are completely dry in summer but flooded during the monsoon rains. A small mango was growing on the island. 'If a small tree can grow here,' said Grandfather, 'so can others.' As soon as the rains set in and while rivers could still be crossed, we set out with a number of tamarind, laburnum, and coral tree saplings and cuttings and spent the day planting them on the island.

The monsoon season was the time for rambling about. At every turn, there was something new to see. Out of the earth and rock and leafless boughs, the magic touch of the rains had brought life and greenness. You could see the broad-leaved vines growing. Plants sprang up in the most unlikely of places. A peepul would take root in the ceiling, a mango would sprout on the window-sill. We did not like to remove them but they had to go if the house was to be kept from falling down.

'If you want to live in a tree, that's all right by me,' said Grandmother crossly. 'But I like having a roof over my head and I'm not going to have my roof brought down by the jungle.'

Then came the Second World War and I was sent away to a boarding school. During the holidays, I went to live with my father in Delhi. Meanwhile, my grandparents sold the house and went to England. Two or three years later, I too went to England and was away from India for several years.

Some years later, I returned to Dehradun. After first visiting the old house – it hadn't changed much – I walked out of town towards the river-bed. It was February. As I looked across the dry water-course, my eye was immediately caught by the spectacular red blooms of the coral blossom. In contrast with the dry river-bed, the island was a small green paradise. When I went up to the trees, I noticed that some squirrels were living in them and a koel, a crow pheasant, challenged me with a mellow 'who-are-you, who-are-you'.

But the trees seemed to know me; they whispered among themselves and beckoned me nearer. And looking around I noticed that other smaller trees, wild plants and grasses had sprung up under their protection. Yes, the trees we had planted long ago had multiplied. They were walking again. In one small corner of the world, Grandfather's dream had come true.

Goodbye, Miss Mackenzie

The Oaks, Holly Mount, The Parsonage, The Pines, Dumbarnie, Mackinnon's Hall, and Windermere. These are names of some of the old houses that still stand on the outskirts of one of the larger Indian hill-stations. They were built over a hundred years ago by British settlers who sought relief from the searing heat of the plains. A few fell into decay and are now inhabited by wild cats, owls, goats, and the occasional mule-driver. Others survive.

Among these old mansions stands a neat, white-washed cottage, Mulberry Lodge. And in it lived an elderly British spinster named Miss Mackenzie.

She was sprightly and wore old-fashioned but well-preserved dresses. Once a week, she walked up to town and bought butter, jam, soap and sometimes a bottle of eau-de-cologne.

Miss Mackenzie had lived there since her teens, before World War I. Her parents, brother, and sister were all dead. She had no relatives in India, and lived on a small pension and gift parcels sent by a childhood friend. She had few visitors – the local padre, the postman, the milkman. Like other lonely old people, she kept a pet, a large black cat with bright, yellow eyes.

In a small garden, she grew dahlias, chrysanthemums, gladioli and a few rare orchids. She knew a great deal about wild flowers, trees, birds, and insects. She never seriously studied them, but had an intimacy with all that grew and flourished around her.

It was September, and the rains were nearly over. Miss Mackenzie's African marigolds were blooming. She hoped the coming winter wouldn't be too severe because she found it increasingly difficult to bear the cold. One day, as she was puttering about in her garden, she saw a schoolboy plucking wild flowers on the slope above the cottage. 'What are you up to, young man?' she called.

Alarmed, the boy tried to dash up the hillside, but slipped on pine needles and slid down the slope into Miss Mackenzie's nasturtium bed. Finding no escape, he gave a bright smile and said, 'Good morning, Miss.'

'Good morning,' said Miss Mackenzie severely. 'Would you mind moving out of my flower bed?'

The boy stepped gingerly over the nasturtiums, and looked at Miss Mackenzie with appealing eyes.

'You ought to be in school,' she said. 'What are you doing here?'

'Picking flowers, Miss.' He held up a bunch of ferns and wild flowers.

'Oh,' Miss Mackenzie was disarmed. It had been a long time since she had seen a boy taking an interest in flowers.

'Do you like flowers?' she asked.

'Yes, Miss. I'm going to be a botan...a botanitist.'

'You mean a botanist?'

'Yes, Miss.'

'That's unusual. Do you know the names of these flowers?'

'This is a buttercup,' he said, showing her a small golden flower. 'But I don't know what this is,' he said, holding out a pale, pink flower with a heart-shaped leaf.

'It's a wild begonia,' said Miss Mackenzie. 'And that purple stuff is salvia. Do you have any books on flowers?'

'No, Miss.'

'Come in and I'll show you one.'

She led the boy into a small front room crowded with furniture, books, vases, and jam jars. He sat awkwardly on the edge of the chair. The cat jumped immediately on to his knees and settled down, purring softly.

'What's your name?' asked Miss Mackenzie, as she rummaged through her books.

'Anil, Miss.'

'And where do you live?'

'When school closes, I go to Delhi. My father has a business there.'

'Oh, and what's that?'

'Bulbs, Miss.'

'Flower bulbs?'

'No, electric bulbs.'

'Ah, here we are!' she said taking a heavy tome from the shelf. '*Flora Himaliensis*, published in 1892, and probably the only copy in India. This is a valuable book, Anil. No other naturalist has recorded as many wild Himalayan flowers. But there are still many plants unknown to the botanists who spend all their time at microscopes instead of in the mountains. Perhaps you'll do something about that one day.'

'Yes, Miss.'

She lit the stove and put the kettle on for tea. And then the old English lady and the small Indian boy sat side by side, absorbed in the book. Miss Mackenzie pointed out many flowers that grew around the hill-station, while the boy made notes of their names and seasons.

'May I come again?' asked Anil, when finally he rose to go.

'If you like,' said Miss Mackenzie. 'But not during school hours. You mustn't miss your classes.'

After that, Anil visited Miss Mackenzie about once a week, and nearly always brought a wild flower for her to identify. She looked forward to the boy's visits. Sometimes when more than a week passed and he didn't come, she would grumble at the cat.

By the middle of October, with only a fortnight left before school closed, snow fell on the distant mountains. One peak stood high above the others, a white pinnacle againt an azure sky. When the sun set, the peak turned from orange to pink to red.

'How high is that mountain?' asked Anil.

'It must be over 15,000 feet,' said Miss Mackenzie. 'I always wanted to go there, but there is no proper road. On the lower slopes, there'll be flowers that you don't get here: blue gentian, purple columbine.'

The day before school closed, Anil came to say goodbye. As he was about to leave, Miss Mackenzie thrust the *Flora Himaliensis* into his hands. 'It's a gift,' she said.

'But I'll be back next year, and I'll be able to look at it then,' he protested. 'Besides, it's so valuable!'

'That's why I'm giving it to you. Otherwise, it will fall into the hands of the junk dealers.'

'But, Miss...'

'Don't argue.'

The boy tucked the book under his arm, stood at attention, and said, 'Goodbye, Miss Mackenzie.' It was the first time he had spoken her name.

Strong winds soon brought rain and sleet, killing the flowers in the garden. The cat stayed indoors, curled up at the foot of the bed. Miss Mackenzie wrapped herself in old shawls and mufflers, but still felt cold. Her fingers grew so stiff that it took almost an hour to open a can of baked beans. Then it snowed, and for several days the milkman did not come.

Tired, she spent most of her time in bed. It was the warmest place. She kept a hot-water bottle against her back, and the cat kept her feet warm. She dreamed of spring and summer. In three months, the primroses would be out, and Anil would return.

One night the hot-water bottle burst, soaking the bed. The sun didn't shine for several days, and the blankets remained damp. Miss Mackenzie caught a chill and had to keep to her cold, uncomfortable bed.

A strong wind sprang up one night and blew the bedroom window open. Miss Mackenzie was too weak to get up and close it. The wind swept the rain and sleet into the room. The cat snuggled close to its mistress's body. Towards morning, the body lost its warmth, and the cat left the bed and started scratching about on the floor.

As sunlight streamed through the window, the milkman arrived. He poured some milk into the saucer on the doorstep, and the cat jumped down from the window-sill.

The milkman called out a greeting to Miss Mackenzie. There was no answer. Knowing she was always up before sunrise, he poked his head in the open window and called again.

Miss Mackenzie did not answer. She had gone to the mountain, where the blue gentian and purple columbine grow.

Pret in the House

It was Grandmother who decided that we must move to another house. And it was all because of a *pret*, a mischievous ghost, who had been making life intolerable for everyone.

In India, *prets* usually live in peepul trees, and that's where our Pret first had his abode – in the branches of an old peepul which had grown through the compound wall and had spread into the garden, on our side, and over the road, on the other side.

For many years, the Pret had lived there quite happily, without bothering anyone in the house. I suppose the traffic on the road had kept him fully occupied. Sometimes, when a *tonga* was passing, he would frighten the pony and, as a result, the little pony-cart would go reeling off the road. Occasionally he would get into the engine of a car or bus, which would soon afterwards have a breakdown. And he liked to knock the sola-topis off the heads of sahibs, who would curse and wonder how a breeze had sprung up so suddenly, only to die down again just as quickly. Although the Pret could make himself felt, and sometimes heard, he was invisible to the human eye.

At night, people avoided walking beneath the peepul tree. It was said that if you yawned beneath the tree, the Pret would jump down your throat and ruin your digestion. Grandmother's tailor, Jaspal, who never had anything ready on time, blamed the Pret for all his troubles. Once, when yawning, Jaspal had forgotten to snap his fingers in front of his mouth – always mandatory when yawning beneath peepul trees – and the Pret had got in without any difficulty. Since then, Jaspal had always been suffering from tummy upsets.

But it had left our family alone until, one day, the peepul tree had been cut down.

It was nobody's fault except, of course, that Grandfather had given the Public Works Department permission to cut the tree which had been standing on our land. They wanted to widen the road, and the tree and a bit of wall were in the way; so both had to go. In any case, not even a ghost can prevail against the PWD. But hardly a day had passed when we discovered that the Pret, deprived of his tree, had decided to take up residence in the bungalow. And since a good Pret must be bad in order to justify his existence, he was soon up to all sorts of mischief in the house.

He began by hiding Grandmother's spectacles whenever she took them off.

'I'm sure I put them down on the dressing-table,' she grumbled.

A little later they were found balanced precariously on the snout of a wild boar, whose stuffed and mounted head adorned the veranda wall. Being the only boy in the house, I was at first blamed for this prank; but a day or two later, when the spectacles disappeared again only to be discovered dangling from the wires of the parrot's cage, it was agreed that some other agency was at work.

Grandfather was the next to be troubled. He went into the garden one morning to find all his prized sweet-peas snipped off and lying on the ground.

Uncle Ken was the next to suffer. He was a heavy sleeper, and once he'd gone to bed, he hated being woken up. So when he came to the breakfast table looking bleary-eyed and miserable, we asked him if he wasn't feeling all right.

'I couldn't sleep a wink last night,' he complained. 'Every time I was about to fall asleep, the bedclothes would be pulled off the bed. I had to get up at least a dozen times to pick them off the floor.' He stared balefully at me. 'Where were you sleeping last night, young man?'

I had an alibi. 'In Grandfather's room,' I said.

'That's right,' said Grandfather. 'And I'm a light sleeper. I'd have woken up if he'd been sleep-walking.'

'It's that ghost from the peepul tree,' said Grandmother.

'It has moved into the house. First my spectacles, then the sweet-peas, and now Ken's bedclothes! What will it be up to next? I wonder!'

We did not have to wonder for long. There followed a series of disasters. Vases fell off tables, pictures came down the walls. Parrot feathers turned up in the teapot while the parrot himself let out indignant squawks in the middle of the night. Uncle Ken found a crow's nest in his bed, and on tossing it out of the window was attacked by two crows.

When Aunt Minnie came to stay, things got worse. The Pret seemed to take an immediate dislike to Aunt Minnie. She was a nervous, easily excitable person, just the right sort of prey for a spiteful ghost. Somehow her toothpaste got switched with a tube of Grandfather's shaving-cream, and when she appeared in the sitting-room, foaming at the mouth, we ran for our lives. Uncle Ken was shouting that she'd got rabies.

Two days later Aunt Minnie complained that she had been hit on the nose by a grapefruit, which had of its own accord taken a leap from the pantry shelf and hurtled across the room straight at her. A bruised and swollen nose testified to the attack. Aunt Minnie swore that life had been more peaceful in Upper Burma.

'We'll have to leave this house,' declared Grandmother.

'If we stay here much longer, both Ken and Minnie will have nervous breakdowns.'

'I thought Aunt Minnie broke down long ago,' I said.

'None of your cheek!' snapped Aunt Minnie.

'Anyway, I agree about changing the house,' I said breezily. 'I can't even do my homework. The ink-bottle is always empty.'

'There was ink in the soup last night.' That came from Grandfather.

And so, a few days and several disasters later, we began moving to a new house.

Two bullock-carts laden with furniture and heavy luggage were sent ahead. The roof of the old car was piled high with bags and kitchen utensils. Everyone squeezed into the car, and Grandfather took the driver's seat.

We were barely out of the gate when we heard a peculiar sound, as if someone was chuckling and talking to himself on the roof of the car.

'Is the parrot out there on the luggage-rack?' the query came from Grandfather.

'No, he's in the cage on one of the bullock-carts,' said Grandmother.

Grandfather stopped the car, got out, and took a look at the roof.

'Nothing up there,' he said, getting in again and starting the engine. 'I'm sure I heard the parrot talking.'

Grandfather had driven some way up the road when the chuckling started again, followed by a squeaky little voice.

We all heard it. It was the Pret talking to itself.

'Let's go, let's go!' it squeaked gleefully. 'A new house. I can't wait to see it. What fun we're going to have!'

The Overcoat

It was clear frosty weather, and as the moon came up over the Himalayan peaks, I could see that patches of snow still lay on the roads of the hill-station. I would have been quite happy in bed, with a book and a hot-water bottle at my side, but I'd promised the Kapadias that I'd go to their party, and I felt it would be churlish of me to stay away. I put on two sweaters, an old football scarf, and an overcoat, and set off down the moonlit road.

It was a walk of just over a mile to the Kapadias' house, and I had covered about half the distance when I saw a girl standing in the middle of the road.

She must have been sixteen or seventeen. She looked rather old-fashioned – long hair, hanging to her waist, and a flummoxy sequined dress, pink and lavender, that reminded me of the photos in my grandmother's family album. When I went closer, I noticed that she had lovely eyes and a winning smile.

'Good evening,' I said. 'It's a cold night to be out.'

'Are you going to the party?' she asked.

'That's right. And I can see from your lovely dress that you're going too. Come along, we're nearly there.'

She fell into step beside me and we soon saw lights from the Kapadias' house shining brightly through the deodars. The girl told me her name was Julie. I hadn't seen her before, but I'd only been in the hill-station a few months.

There was quite a crowd at the party, and no one seemed to know Julie. Everyone thought she was a friend of mine. I did not deny it. Obviously she was someone who was feeling lonely and wanted to be friendly with people. And she was certainly enjoying herself. I did not see her do much eating or drinking, but she flitted about from one group to another, talking, listening, laughing; and when the music began, she was dancing almost continuously, alone or with partners, it didn't matter which, she was completely wrapped up in the music.

It was almost midnight when I got up to go. I had drunk a fair amount of punch, and I was ready for bed. As I was saying goodnight to my hosts and wishing everyone a merry Christmas, Julie slipped her arm into mine and said she'd be going home too.

When we were outside, I said, 'Where do you live, Julie?'

'At Wolfsburn,' she said. 'Right at the top of the hill.'

'There's a cold wind,' I said. 'And although your dress is beautiful, it doesn't look very warm. Here, you'd better wear my overcoat. I've plenty of protection.'

She did not protest, and allowed me to slip my overcoat over her shoulders. Then we started out on the walk home. But I did not have to escort her all the way. At about the spot where we had met, she said, 'There's a short cut from here. I'll just scramble up the hillside.'

'Do you know it well?' I asked. 'It's a very narrow path.'

'Oh, I know every stone on the path. I use it all the time. And besides, it's a really bright night.'

'Well, keep the coat on,' I said. 'I can collect it tomorrow.'

She hesitated for a moment, then smiled and nodded. She then disappeared up the hill, and I went home alone.

The next day I walked up to Wolfsburn. I crossed a little brook, from which the house had probably got its name, and entered an open iron gate. But of the house itself, little remained. Just a roofless ruin, a pile of stones, a shattered chimney, a few Doric pillars where a veranda had once stood.

Had Julie played a joke on me? Or had I found the wrong house?

I walked around the hill, to the mission house where the Taylors lived and asked old Mrs Taylor if she knew a girl called Julie.

'No, I don't think so,' she said. 'Where does she live?'

'At Wolfsburn, I was told. But the house is just a ruin.'

'Nobody has lived at Wolfsburn for over forty years. The Mackinnons lived there. One of the old families who settled here. But when their girl died...' She stopped and gave me a queer look. 'I think her name was Julie...Anyway, when she died, they sold the house and went away. No one ever lived in it again, and it fell into decay. But it couldn't be the same Julie you're looking for. She died of consumption – there wasn't much you could do about it in those days. Her grave is in the cemetery, just down the road.'

I thanked Mrs Taylor and walked slowly down the road to the cemetery; not really wanting to know any more, but propelled forward almost against my will.

It was a small cemetery under the deodars. You could see the eternal snows of the Himalayas standing out against the pristine blue of the sky. Here lay the bones of forgotten empire-builders – soldiers, merchants, adventurers, their wives and children. It did not take me long to find Julie's grave. It had a simple headstone with her name clearly outlined on it:

Julie Mackinnon
1923-39
'With us one moment,
Taken the next,
Gone to her Maker,
Gone to her rest.'

Although many monsoons had swept across the cemetery wearing down the stones, they had not touched this little tombstone.

I was turning to leave when I caught a glimpse of something familiar behind the headstone. I walked round to where it lay.

Neatly folded on the grass was my overcoat.

No thank-you note. But something soft and invisible brushed against my cheek, and I knew someone was trying to thank me.

The Tunnel

It was almost noon, and the jungle was very still, very silent. Heat waves shimmered along the railway embankment where it cut a path through the tall evergreen trees. The railway lines were two straight black serpents disappearing into the tunnel in the hillside.

Suraj stood near the cutting, waiting for the mid-day train. It wasn't a station, and he wasn't catching a train. He was waiting so that he could watch the steam-engine come roaring out of the tunnel.

He had cycled out of the town and taken the jungle path until he had come to a small village.

He had left the cycle there, and walked over a low, scrub-covered hill and down to the tunnel exit.

Now he looked up. He had heard, in the distance, the shrill whistle of the engine. He couldn't see anything, because the train was approaching from the other side of the hill; but presently a sound, like distant thunder, issued from the tunnel, and he knew the train was coming through.

A second or two later, the steam-engine shot out of the tunnel, snorting and puffing like some green, black and gold dragon, some beautiful monster out of Suraj's dreams. Showering sparks left and right, it roared a challenge to the jungle.

Instinctively, Suraj stepped back a few paces. And then the train had gone, leaving only a plume of smoke to drift lazily over tall *shisham* trees.

The jungle was still again. No one moved. Suraj turned from his contemplation of the drifting smoke and began walking along the embankment towards the tunnel.

The tunnel grew darker as he walked further into it. When he had gone about twenty yards, it became pitch black. Suraj had to turn and look back at the opening to reassure himself that there was still daylight outside. Ahead of him, the tunnel's other opening was just a small round circle of light.

The tunnel was still full of smoke from the train, but it would be several hours before another train came through. Till then, it belonged to the jungle again.

Suraj didn't stop, because there was nothing to do in the tunnel and nothing to see. He had simply wanted to walk through, so that he would know what the inside of a tunnel was really like. The walls were damp and sticky. A bat flew past. A lizard scuttled between the lines.

Coming straight from the darkness into the light, Suraj was dazzled by the sudden glare. He put a hand up to shade his eyes and looked up at the tree-covered hillside. He thought he saw something moving between the trees.

It was just a flash of orange and gold, and a long swishing tail. It was there between the trees for a second or two, and then it was gone.

About fifty feet from the entrance to the tunnel stood the watchman's hut. Marigolds grew in front of the hut, and at the back there was a small vegetable patch. It was the watchman's duty to inspect the tunnel and keep it clear of obstacles. Every day, before the train came through, he would walk the length of the tunnel. If all was well, he would return to his hut and take a nap. If something was wrong, he would walk back up the line and wave a red flag and the engine-driver would slow down. At night, the watchman lit an oil lamp and made a similar inspection of the tunnel. Of course, he could not stop the train if there was a porcupine on the line. But if there was any danger to the train, he'd go back up the line and wave his lamp to the approaching engine. If all was well, he'd hang his lamp at the door of the hut and go to sleep.

He was just settling down on his cot for an afternoon nap when he saw the boy emerge from the tunnel. He waited until Suraj was only a few feet away and then said: 'Welcome, welcome, I don't often have visitors. Sit down for a while, and tell me why you were inspecting my tunnel.'

'Is it your tunnel?' asked Suraj.

'It is,' said the watchman. 'It is truly my tunnel, since no one else will have anything to do with it. I have only lent it to the government.'

Suraj sat down on the edge of the cot.

'I wanted to see the train come through,' he said. 'And then, when it had gone, I thought I'd walk through the tunnel.'

'And what did you find in it?'

'Nothing. It was very dark. But when I came out, I thought I saw an animal – up on the hill – but I'm not sure, it moved away very quickly.'

'It was a leopard you saw,' said the watchman. 'My leopard.'

'Do you own a leopard too?'

'I do.'

'And do you lend it to the government?'

'I do not.'

'Is it dangerous?'

'No, it's a leopard that minds its own business. It comes to this range for a few days every month.'

'Have you been here a long time?' asked Suraj.

'Many years. My name is Sunder Singh.'

'My name's Suraj.'

'There's one train during the day. And another during the night. Have you seen the night mail come through the tunnel?'

'No. At what time does it come?'

'About nine o'clock, if it isn't late. You could come and sit here with me, if you like. And after it has gone, I'll take you home.'

'I shall ask my parents,' said Suraj. 'Will it be safe?'

'Of course. It's safer in the jungle than in the town. Nothing happens to me out here, but last month when I went into the town, I was almost run over by a bus.'

Sunder Singh yawned and stretched himself out on the cot. 'And now I'm going to take a nap, my friend. It is too hot to be up and about in the afternoon.'

'Everyone goes to sleep in the afternoon,' complained Suraj. 'My father lies down as soon as he's had his lunch.'

'Well, the animals also rest in the heat of the day. It is only the tribe of boys who cannot, or will not, rest.'

Sunder Singh placed a large banana-leaf over his face to keep away the flies, and was soon snoring gently. Suraj stood up, looking up and down the railway tracks. Then he began walking back to the village.

The following evening, towards dusk, as the flying foxes swooped silently out of the trees, Suraj made his way to the watchman's hut.

It had been a long hot day, but now the earth was cooling, and a light breeze was moving through the trees. It carried with it a scent of mango blossoms, the promise of rain.

Sunder Singh was waiting for Suraj. He had watered his small garden, and the flowers looked cool and fresh. A kettle was boiling on a small oil-stove.

'I'm making tea,' he said. 'There's nothing like a glass of hot tea while waiting for a train.'

They drank their tea, listening to the sharp notes of the tailorbird and the noisy chatter of the seven-sisters. As the brief twilight faded, most of the birds fell silent. Sunder Singh lit his oil-lamp and said it was time for him to inspect the tunnel. He moved off towards the tunnel, while Suraj sat on the cot, sipping his tea. In the dark, the trees seemed to move closer to him. And the night life of the forest was conveyed on the breeze – the sharp call of a barking-deer, the cry of a fox, the quaint *tonk-tonk* of a nightjar. There were some sounds that Suraj couldn't recognise – sounds that came from the trees, creakings and whisperings, as though the trees were coming alive, stretching their limbs in the dark, shifting a little, reflexing their fingers.

Sunder Singh stood inside the tunnel, trimming his lamp. The night sounds were familiar to him and he did not give them much thought; but something else – a padded footfall, a rustle of dry leaves – made him stand alert for a few seconds, peering into the darkness. Then, humming softly to himself, he returned to where Suraj was waiting. Another ten minutes remained for the night mail to arrive.

As Sunder Singh sat down on the cot beside Suraj, a new sound reached both of them quite distinctly – a rhythmic sawing sound, as if someone was cutting through the branch of a tree.

'What's that?' whispered Suraj.

'It's the leopard,' said Sunder Singh.

'I think it's in the tunnel.'

'The train will soon be here,' reminded Suraj.

'Yes, my friend. And if we don't drive the leopard out of the tunnel, it will be run over and killed. I can't let that happen.'

'But won't it attack us if we try to drive it out?' asked Suraj, beginning to share the watchman's concern.

'Not this leopard. It knows me well. We have seen each other many times. It has a weakness for goats and stray dogs, but it won't harm us. Even so, I'll take my axe with me. You stay here, Suraj.'

'No, I'm going with you. It'll be better than sitting here alone in the dark!'

'All right, but stay close behind me. And remember, there's nothing to fear.'

Raising his lamp high, Sunder Singh advanced into the tunnel, shouting at the top of his voice to try and scare away the animal. Suraj followed close behind, but he found he was unable to do any shouting. His throat was quite dry.

They had gone just about twenty paces into the tunnel when the light from the lamp fell upon the leopard. It was crouching between the tracks, only fifteen feet away from them. It was not a very big leopard, but it looked lithe and sinewy. Baring its teeth and snarling, it went down on its belly, tail twitching.

Suraj and Sunder Singh both shouted together. Their voices rang through the tunnel. And the leopard, uncertain as to how many terrifying humans were there in the tunnel with him, turned swiftly and disappeared into the darkness.

To make sure that it had gone, Sunder Singh and Suraj walked the length of the tunnel. When they returned to the entrance, the rails were beginning to hum. They knew the train was coming.

Suraj put his hand to the rails and felt its tremor. He heard the distant rumble of the train. And then the engine came round the bend, hissing at them, scattering sparks into the darkness, defying the jungle as it roared through the steep sides of the cutting. It charged straight at the tunnel, and into it, thundering past Suraj like the beautiful dragon of his dreams.

And when it had gone, the silence returned and the forest seemed to breathe, to live again. Only the rails still trembled with the passing of the train.

And they trembled to the passing of the same train, almost a week later, when Suraj and his father were both travelling in it.

Suraj's father was scribbling in a notebook, doing his accounts. Suraj sat at an open window staring out at the darkness. His father was going to Delhi on a business trip and had decided to take the boy along. ('I don't know where he gets to, most of the time,' he'd complained. 'I think it's time he learnt something about my business.')

The night mail rushed through the forest with its hundreds of passengers. Tiny flickering lights came and went, as they passed small villages on the fringe of the jungle.

Suraj heard the rumble as the train passed over a small bridge. It was too dark to see the hut near the cutting, but he knew they must be approaching the tunnel. He strained his eyes looking out into the night; and then, just as the engine let out a shrill whistle, Suraj saw the lamp.

He couldn't see Sunder Singh, but he saw the lamp, and he knew that his friend was out there.

The train went into the tunnel and out again; it left the jungle behind and thundered across the endless plains; and Suraj stared out at the darkness, thinking of the lonely cutting in the forest, and the watchman with the lamp who would always remain a firefly for those travelling thousands, as he lit up the darkness for steam-engines and leopards.

Wild Fruit

It was a long walk to school. Down the hill, through the rhododendron trees, across a small stream, around a bare, brown hill, and then through the narrow little bazaar, past fruit stalls piled high with oranges, guavas, bananas, and apples.

The boy's gaze often lingered on those heaps of golden oranges – oranges grown in the plains, now challenging the pale winter sunshine in the hills. His nose twitched at the sharp smell of melons in summer; his fingers would sometimes touch for a moment the soft down on the skin of a peach. But these were forbidden fruit. The boy hadn't the money for them.

He took one meal at seven in the morning when he left home; another at seven in the evening when he returned from school. There were times – especially when he was at school, and his teacher droned on and on, lecturing on honesty, courage, duty, and self-sacrifice – when he felt very hungry; but on the way to school, or on the way home, there was nearly always the prospect of some wild fruit.

The boy's name was Vijay, and he belonged to a village near Mussoorie. His parents tilled a few narrow terraces on the hill slopes. They grew potatoes, onions, barley, maize; barely enough to feed themselves. When greens were scarce, they boiled the tops of the stinging-nettle and made them into a dish resembling spinach.

Vijay's parents realised the importance of sending him to school, and it didn't cost them much, except for the books. But it was all of four miles to the town, and a long walk makes a boy hungry.

But there was nearly always the wild fruit. The purple berries of the thorny bilberry bushes, ripening in May and June. Wild strawberries, growing in shady places like spots of blood on the deep green monsoon grass. Small, sour cherries, and tough medlars. Vijay's strong teeth and probing tongue extracted whatever tang or sweetness lay hidden in them. And in March there were the rhododendron flowers.

His mother made them into jam. But Vijay liked them as they were. He placed the petals on his tongue and chewed them till the sweet juice trickled down his throat. But in November, there was no wild fruit. Only acorns on the oak trees, and they were bitter, fit only for the monkeys.

He walked confidently through the bazaar, strong in the legs. He looked a healthy boy, until you came up close and saw the patches on his skin and the dullness in his eyes.

He passed the fruit stalls, wondering who ate all that fruit, and what happened to the fruit that went bad; he passed the sweet shop, where hot, newly-fried *jelabies* lay protected like twisted orange jewels in a glass case, and where a fat, oily man raised a knife and plunged it deep into a thick slab of rich amber-coloured *halwa*.

The saliva built up in Vijay's mouth; there was a dull ache in his stomach. But his eyes gave away nothing of the sharp pangs he felt.

And now, a confectioner's shop. Glass jars filled with chocolates, peppermints, toffees – sweets he didn't know the names of, English sweets – wrapped in bits of coloured paper.

A boy had just bought a bag of sweets. He had one in his mouth. He was a well-dressed boy; coins jingled in his pocket. The sweet moved from one cheek to the other. He bit deep into it, and Vijay heard the crunch and looked up. The boy smiled at Vijay, but moved away.

They met again, further along the road. Once again the boy smiled, even looked as though he was about to offer Vijay a sweet; but this time, Vijay shyly looked away. He did not want it to appear that he had noticed the sweets, or that he hungered for one.

But he kept meeting the boy, who always managed to reappear at some corner, sucking a sweet, moving it about in his mouth, letting it show between his wet lips – a sticky green thing, temptingly, lusciously beautiful.

The bag of sweets was nearly empty.

Reluctantly, Vijay decided that he must overtake the boy, forget all about the sweets, and hurry home. Otherwise, he would be tempted to grab the bag and run!

And then, he saw the boy leave the bag on a bench, look at him once, and smile – smile shyly and invitingly – before moving away.

Was the bag empty? Vijay wondered with mounting excitement. It couldn't be, or it would have blown away almost immediately. Obviously, there were still a few sweets in it. The boy had disappeared. He had gone for his tea, and Vijay could have the rest of the sweets.

Vijay took the bag and jammed it into a pocket of his shirt. Then he hurried homewards. It was getting late, and he wanted to be home before dark.

As soon as he was out of the town, he opened the bag and shook the sweets out. Their red wrappers glowed like rubies in the palm of his hand.

Carefully, he undid a wrapper.

There was no sweet inside, only a smooth, round stone.

Vijay found stones in all the wrappers. In his mind's eye, Vijay saw the smiling face of the boy in the bazaar: a boy who smiled sweetly but exchanged stones for sweets.

Forcing back angry tears, Vijay flung the stones down the hillside. Then he shouldered his bag of books and began the long walk home.

There were patches of snow on the ground. The grass was a dirty brown, the bushes were bare.

There is no wild fruit in November.

The Night the Roof Blew Off

We are used to sudden storms, up here on the first range of the Himalayas. The old building in which we live has, for more than a hundred years, received the full force of the wind as it sweeps across the hills from the east.

We'd lived in the building for more than ten years without a disaster. It had even taken the shock of a severe earthquake. As my granddaughter Dolly said, 'It's difficult to tell the new cracks from the old!'

It's a two-storey building, and I live on the upper floor with my family: my three grandchildren and their parents. The roof is made of corrugated tin sheets, the ceiling of wooden boards. That's the traditional Mussoorie roof.

Looking back at the experience, it was the sort of thing that should have happened in a James Thurber story, like the dam that burst or the ghost who got in. But I wasn't thinking of Thurber at the time, although a few of his books were among the many I was trying to save from the icy rain pouring into my bedroom.

Our roof had held fast in many a storm, but the wind that night was really fierce. It came rushing at us with a high-pitched, eerie wail. The old roof groaned and protested. It took a battering for several hours while the rain lashed against the windows and the lights kept coming and going.

There was no question of sleeping, but we remained in bed for warmth and comfort. The fire had long since gone out, as the chimney had collapsed, bringing down a shower of sooty rainwater.

After about four hours of buffeting, the roof could take it no longer. My bedroom faces east, so my portion of the roof was the first to go.

The wind got under it and kept pushing until, with a ripping, groaning sound, the metal sheets shifted and slid off the rafters, some of them dropping with claps like thunder on to the road below.

So that's it, I thought. Nothing worse can happen. As long as the ceiling stays on, I'm not getting out of bed. We'll collect our roof in the morning.

Icy water splashing down on my face made me change my mind in a hurry. Leaping from the bed, I found that much of the ceiling had gone, too. Water was pouring on my open typewriter as well as on the bedside radio and bed cover.

Picking up my precious typewriter (my companion for forty years) I stumbled into the front sitting room (and library), only to find a similar situation there. Water was pouring through the slats of the wooden ceiling, raining down on the open bookshelves.

By now I had been joined by the children, who had come to my rescue. Their section of the roof hadn't gone as yet. Their parents were struggling to close a window against the driving rain.

'Save the books!' shouted Dolly, the youngest, and that became our rallying cry for the next hour or two.

Dolly and her brother Mukesh picked up armfuls of books and carried them into their room. But the floor was awash, so the books had to be piled on their beds. Dolly was helping me gather some of my papers when a large field rat jumped on to the desk in front of her. Dolly squealed and ran for the door.

'It's all right,' said Mukesh, whose love of animals extends even to field rats. 'It's only sheltering from the storm.'

Big brother Rakesh whistled for our dog, Tony, but Tony wasn't interested in rats just then. He had taken shelter in the kitchen, the only dry spot in the house.

Two rooms were now practically roofless, and we could see the sky lit up by flashes of lightning.

There were fireworks indoors, too, as water spluttered and crackled along a damaged wire. Then the lights went out altogether.

Rakesh, at his best in an emergency, had already lit two kerosene lamps. And by their light we continued to transfer books, papers, and clothes to the children's room.

We noticed that the water on the floor was beginning to subside a little.

'Where is it going?' asked Dolly.

'Through the floor,' said Mukesh. 'Down to the flat below!'

Cries of concern from our downstairs neighbours told us that they were having their share of the flood.

Our feet were freezing because there hadn't been time to put on proper footwear. And besides, shoes and slippers were awash by now. All chairs and tables were piled high with books. I hadn't realised the extent of my library until that night!

The available beds were pushed into the driest corner of the children's room, and there, huddled in blankets and quilts, we spent the remaining hours of the night while the storm continued.

Towards morning the wind fell, and it began to snow. Through the door to the sitting room I could see snowflakes drifting through the gaps in the ceiling, settling on picture-frames. Ordinary things like a glue bottle and a small clock took on a certain beauty when covered with soft snow.

Most of us dozed off.

When dawn came, we found the windowpanes encrusted with snow and icicles. The rising sun struck through the gaps in the ceiling and turned everything golden. Snow crystals glistened on the empty bookshelves. But the books had been saved.

Rakesh went out to find a carpenter and tinsmith, while the rest of us started putting things in the sun to dry. By evening we'd put much of the roof back on.

It's a much-improved roof now, and we look forward to the next storm with confidence!

A Traveller's Tale

Gopalpur-on-sea!

A name to conjure with... And as a boy I'd heard it mentioned, by my father and others, and described as a quaint little seaside resort with a small port on the Orissa coast. The years passed, and I went from boyhood to manhood and eventually old age (is seventy-six old age? I wouldn't know) and still it was only a place I'd heard about and dreamt about but never visited.

Until last month, when I was a guest of KiiT International School in Bhubaneswar, and someone asked me where I'd like to go, and I said, 'Is Gopalpur very far?'

'And off I went, along a plam-fringed highway, through busy little market-towns with names Rhamba and Humma, past the enormous Chilika Lake which opens into the sea through paddy fields and keora plantations, and finally on to Gopalpur's beach road, with the sun glinting like gold on the great waves of the ocean, and the fishermen counting their catch, and the children sprinting into the sea, tumbling about in the shallows.

But the seafront wore a neglected look. The hotels were empty, the cafés deserted. A cheeky crow greeted me with a disconsolate caw from its perch on a weathered old wall. Some of the buildings were recent, but around us there were also the shells of older buildings that had fallen into ruin. And no one was going to preserve these relics of a colonial past. A small house called 'Brighton Villa' still survived.

But away from the seafront a tree-lined road took us past some well-maintained bungalows, a school, an old cemetery, and finally a PWD rest house where we were to spend the night.

It was growing dark when we arrived, and in the twilight I could just make out the shapes of the trees that surround the old bungalow – a hoary old banyan, a jack-fruit and several mango trees. The light from the bungalow's veranda fell on some oleander bushes. A hawk moth landed on my shirt-front and appeared reluctant to leave. I took it between my fingers and deposited it on the oleander bush.

It was almost midnight when I went to bed. The rest-house staff – the caretaker and the gardener – went to some trouble to arrange a meal, but it was a long time coming. The gardener told me the house had once been the residence of an Englishman who had left the country at the time of Independence, some sixty years or more ago. Some changes had been carried out, but the basic structure remained – high-ceilinged rooms with skylights, a long veranda and enormous bathrooms. The bathroom was so large you could have held a party in it. But there was just one potty and a basin. You could sit on the potty and meditate, fixing your thoughts (or absence of thought) on the distant basin.

I closed all doors and windows, switched off all lights (I find it impossible to sleep with a light on), and went to bed.

It was a comfortable bed, and I soon fell asleep. Only to be awakened by a light tapping on the window near my bed.

Probably a branch of the oleander bush, I thought, and fell asleep again. But there was more tapping, louder this time, and then I was fully awake.

I sat up in bed and drew aside the curtains.

There was a face at the window.

In the half-light from the veranda I could not make out the features, but it was definitely a human face.

Obviously someone wanted to come in, the caretaker perhaps, or the chowkidar. But then, why not knock on the door? Perhaps he had. The door was at the other end of the room, and I may not have heard the knocking.

I am not in the habit of opening my doors to strangers in the night, but somehow I did not feel threatened or uneasy, so I got up, unlatched the door, and opened it for my midnight visitor.

Standing on the threshold was an imposing figure.

A tall dark man, turbaned, and dressed all in white. He wore some sort of uniform – the kind worn by those immaculate doormen at five-star hotels; but a rare sight in Gopalpur-on-sea.

'What is it you want?' I asked. 'Are you staying here?'

He did not reply but looked past me, possibly through me, and then walked silently into the room. I stood there, bewildered and awestruck, as he strode across to my bed, smoothed out the sheets and patted down my pillow. He then walked over to the next room and came back with a glass and a jug of water, which he placed on the bedside table. As if that were not enough, he picked up my day clothes, folded them neatly and placed them on a vacant chair. Then, just as unobtrusively and without so much as a glance in my direction, he left the room and walked out into the night.

Early next morning, as the sun came up like thunder over the Bay of Bengal, I went down to the sea again, picking my way over the puddles of human excreta that decorated parts of the beach. Well, you can't have everything. The world might be more beautiful without the human presence; but then, who would appreciate it?

Back at the rest house for breakfast, I was reminded of my visitor of the previous night.

'Who was the tall gentleman who came to my room last night?' I asked. 'He looked like a butler. Smartly dressed, very dignified.'

The caretaker and the gardener exchanged meaningful glances.

'You tell him,' said the caretaker to his companion.

'It must have been Hazoor Ali,' said the gardener, nodding. 'He was the orderly, the personal servant of Mr Robbins, the port commissioner – the Englishman who lived here.'

'But that was over sixty years ago,' I said. 'They must all be dead.'

'Yes, all are dead, sir. But sometimes the ghost of Hazoor Ali appears, especially if one of our guests reminds him of his old master. He was quite devoted to him, sir. In fact, he received this bungalow as a parting gift when Mr Robbins left the country. But unable to maintain it, he sold it to the government and returned to his home in Cuttack. He died many years ago, but revisits this place sometimes. Do not feel alarmed, sir. He means no harm. And he does not appear to everyone – you are the lucky one this year! I have but seen him twice. Once, when I took service here twenty years ago, and then, last year, the night before the cyclone. He came to warn us, I think. Went to every door and window and made sure they were secured. Never said a word. Just vanished into the night.'

'And it's time for me to vanish by day,' I said, getting my things ready. I had to be in Bhubaneswar by late afternoon, to board the plane for Delhi. I was sorry it had been such a short stay. I would have liked to spend a few days in Gopalpur, wandering about its backwaters, old roads, mango groves, fishing villages, sandy inlets... Another time perhaps. In this life, if I am so lucky. Or the next, if I am luckier still.

At the airport in Bhubaneswar, the security asked me for my photo-identity. 'Driving licence, pan card, passport? Anything with your picture on it will do, since you have an e-ticket,' he explained.

I do not have a driving licence and have never felt the need to carry my pan card with me. Luckily, I always carry my passport on my travels. I looked for it in my little travel-bag and then in my suitcase, but couldn't find it. I was feeling awkward fumbling in all my pockets, when another senior officer came to my rescue. 'It's all right. Let him in. I know Mr Ruskin Bond,' he called out, and beckoned me inside. I thanked him and hurried into the check-in area.

All the time in the flight, I was trying to recollect where I might have kept my passport. Possibly tucked away somewhere inside the suitcase, I thought. Now that my baggage was sealed at the airport, I decided to look for it when I reached home.

A day later I was back in my home in the hills, tired after a long road journey from Delhi. I like travelling by road, there is so much to see, but the ever-increasing volume of traffic turns it into an obstacle race most of the time. To add to my woes, my passport was still missing. I looked for it everywhere – my suitcase, travel-bag, in all my pockets.

I gave up the search. Either I had dropped it somewhere, or I had left it at Gopalpur. I decided to ring up and check with the rest house staff the next day.

It was a frosty night, bitingly cold, so I went to bed early, well-covered with *razai* and blanket. Only two nights previously I had been sleeping under a fan!

It was a windy night, the windows were rattling; and the old tin roof was groaning, a loose sheet flapping about and making a frightful din.

I slept only fitfully.

When the wind abated, I heard someone knocking on my front door.

'Who's there?' I called, but there was no answer.

The knocking continued, insistent, growing louder all the time.

'Who's there? *Kaun hai*?' I call again.

Only that knocking.

Someone in distress, I thought. I'd better see who it is. I got up shivering, and walked barefoot to the front door. Opened it slowly, opened it wider, someone stepped out of the shadows.

Hazoor Ali salaamed, entered the room, and as in Gopalpur, he walked silently into the room. It was lying in disarray because of my frantic search for my passport. He arranged the room, removed my garments from my travel-bag, folded them and placed them neatly upon the cupboard shelves. Then, he did a salaam again and waited at the door.

Strange, I thought. If he did the entire room why did he not set the travel-bag in its right place? Why did he leave it lying on the floor? Possibly he didn't know where to keep it; he left the last bit of work for me. I picked up the bag to place it on the top shelf. And there, from its front pocket my passport fell out, on to the floor.

I turned to look at Hazoor Ali, but he had already walked out into the cold darkness.

And Now We are Twelve

People often ask me why I've chosen to live in Mussoorie for so long – almost forty years, without any significant breaks.

'I forgot to go away,' I tell them, but of course, that isn't the real reason.

The people here are friendly, but then people are friendly in a great many other places. The hills, the valleys are beautiful; but they are just as beautiful in Kulu or Kumaon.

'This is where the family has grown up and where we all live,' I say, and those who don't know me are puzzled because the general impression of the writer is of a reclusive old bachelor.

Unmarried I may be, but single I am not. Not since Prem came to live and work with me in 1970. A year later, he was married. Then his children came along and stole my heart; and when they grew up, their children came along and stole my wits. So now I'm an enchanted bachelor, head of a family of twelve. Sometimes I go out to bat, sometimes to bowl, but generally I prefer to be twelfth man, carrying out the drinks.

In the old days, when I was a solitary writer living on baked beans, the prospect of my suffering from obesity was very remote. Now there is a little more of author than there used to be, and the other day five-year-old Gautam patted me on my tummy (or balcony, as I prefer to call it) and remarked; 'Dada, you should join the WWF.'

'I'm already a member,' I said, 'I joined the World Wildlife Fund years ago.'

'Not that,' he said. 'I mean the World Wrestling Federation.'

If I have a tummy today, it's thanks to Gautam's grandfather and now his mother who, over the years, have made sure that I am well-fed and well-proportioned.

Forty years ago, when I was a lean young man, people would look at me and say, 'Poor chap, he's definitely undernourished. What on earth made him take up writing as a profession?' Now they look at me and say, 'You wouldn't think he was a writer, would you? Too well nourished!'

✧

It was a cold, wet and windy March evening when Prem came back from the village with his wife and first-born child, then just four months old. In those days, they had to walk to the house from the bus stand; it was a half-hour walk in the cold rain, and the baby was all wrapped up when they entered the front room. Finally, I got a glimpse of him. And he of me, and it was friendship at first sight. Little Rakesh (as he was to be called) grabbed me by the nose and held on. He did not have much of a nose to grab, but he had a dimpled chin and I played with it until he smiled.

The little chap spent a good deal of his time with me during those first two years in Maplewood – learning to crawl, to toddle, and then to walk unsteadily about the little sitting-room. I would carry him into the garden, and later, up the steep gravel path to the main road. Rakesh enjoyed these little excursions, and so did I, because in pointing out trees, flowers, birds, butterflies, beetles, grasshoppers, *et al*, I was giving myself a chance to observe them better instead of just taking them for granted.

In particular, there was a pair of squirrels that lived in the big oak tree outside the cottage. Squirrels are rare in Mussoorie though common enough down in the valley. This couple must have come up for the summer. They became quite friendly, and although they never got around to taking food from our hands, they were soon entering the house quite freely. The sitting room window opened directly on to the oak tree whose various denizens – ranging from stag-beetles to small birds and even an acrobatic bat – took to darting in and out of the cottage at various times of the day or night.

Life at Maplewood was quite idyllic, and when Rakesh's baby brother, Suresh, came into the world, it seemed we were all set for a long period of domestic bliss; but at such times tragedy is often lurking just around the corner. Suresh was just over a year old when he contracted tetanus. Doctors and hospitals were of no avail. He suffered – as any child would from this terrible affliction – and left this world before he had a chance of getting to know it. His parents were broken-hearted. And I feared for Rakesh, for he wasn't a very healthy boy, and two of his cousins in the village had already succumbed to tuberculosis.

It was to be a difficult year for me. A criminal charge was brought against me for a slightly risqué story I'd written for a Bombay magazine. I had to face trial in Bombay and this involved three journeys there over a period of a year and a half, before an irate but perceptive judge found the charges baseless and gave me an honourable acquittal.

It's the only time I've been involved with the law and I sincerely hope it is the last. Most cases drag on interminably, and the main beneficiaries are the lawyers. My trial would have been much longer had not the prosecutor died of a heart attack in the middle of the proceedings. His successor did not pursue it with the same vigour. His heart was not in it. The whole issue had started with a complaint by a local politician, and when he lost interest so did the prosecution. Nevertheless the trial, once begun, had to be seen through. The defence (organised by the concerned magazine) marshalled its witnesses (which included Nissim Ezekiel and the Marathi playwright Vijay Tendulkar). I made a short speech which couldn't have been very memorable as I have forgotten it! And everyone, including the judge, was bored with the whole business. After that, I steered clear of controversial publications. I have never set out to shock the world. Telling a meaningful story was all that really mattered. And that is still the case.

I was looking forward to continuing our idyllic existence in Maplewood, but it was not to be. The powers-that-be, in the shape of the Public Works Department (PWD), had decided to build a 'strategic' road just below the cottage and without any warning to us, all the trees in the vicinity were felled (including the friendly old oak) and the hillside was rocked by explosives and bludgeoned by bulldozers. I decided it was time to move. Prem and Chandra (Rakesh's mother) wanted to move too; not because of the road, but because they associated the house with the death of little Suresh, whose presence seemed to haunt every room, every corner of the cottage. His little cries of pain and suffering still echoed through the still hours of the night.

I rented rooms at the top of Landour, a good thousand feet higher up the mountain. Rakesh was now old enough to go to school, and every morning I would walk with him down to the little convent school near the clock tower. Prem would go to fetch him in the afternoon. The walk took us about half-an-hour, and on the way Rakesh would ask for a story and I would have to rack my brains in order to invent one. I am not the most inventive of writers, and fantastical plots are beyond me. My forte is observation, recollection, and reflection. Small boys prefer action. So I invented a leopard who suffered from acute indigestion because he'd eaten one human too many and a belt buckle was causing an obstruction.

This went down quite well until Rakesh asked me how the leopard got around the problem of the victim's clothes.

'The secret,' I said, 'is to pounce on them when their trousers are off!'

Not the stuff of which great picture books are made, but then, I've never attempted to write stories for beginners. Red Riding Hood's granny-eating wolf always scared me as a small boy, and yet parents have always found it acceptable for toddlers. Possibly they feel grannies are expendable.

Mukesh was born around this time and Savitri (Dolly) a couple of years later. When Dolly grew older, she was annoyed at having been named Savitri (my choice), which is now considered very old-fashioned; so we settled for Dolly. I can understand a child's dissatisfaction with given names.

My first name was Owen, which in Welsh means 'brave'. As I am not in the least brave, I have preferred not to use it. One given name and one surname should be enough.

When my granny said, 'But you should try to be brave, otherwise how will you survive in this cruel world?' I replied: 'Don't worry, I can run very fast.'

Not that I've ever had to do much running, except when I was pursued by a lissome Australian lady who thought I'd make a good obedient husband. It wasn't so much the lady I was running from, but the prospect of spending the rest of my life in some remote cattle station in the Australian outback. Anyone who has tried to drag me away from India has always met with stout resistance.

✧

Up on the heights of Landour lived a motley crowd. My immediate neighbours included a Frenchwoman who played the sitar (very badly) all through the night; and a Spanish lady with two husbands, one of whom practised acupuncture – rather ineffectively as far as he was concerned, for he seemed to be dying of some mysterious debilitating disease. Another neighbour came and went rather mysteriously, and finally ended up in Tihar jail, having been apprehended at Delhi carrying a large amount of contraband hashish.

Apart from these and a few other colourful characters, the area was inhabitated by some very respectable people, retired brigadiers, air marshals and rear admirals, almost all of whom were busy writing their memoirs. I had to read or listen to extracts from their literary efforts. This was slow torture. A few years before, I had done a stint of editing for a magazine called *Imprint.* It had involved going through hundreds of badly written manuscripts, and in some cases (friends of the owner!) rewriting some of them for publication. One of life's joys had been to throw up that particular job, and now here I was, besieged by all the top brass of the army, navy and air force, each one determined that I should read, inwardly digest, improve, and if possible find a publisher for their outpourings. Thank goodness they were all retired. I could not be shot or court-martialled. But at least two of them set their wives upon me, and these intrepid ladies would turn up around noon with my 'homework' – typescripts to read and edit! There was no escape. My own writing was of no consequence to them. I told them that I was taking sitar lessons, but they disapproved, saying I was more suited to the tabla.

When Prem discovered a set of vacant rooms further down the Landour slope, close to school and bazaar, I rented them without hesitation. This was Ivy Cottage. Come up and see me sometime, but leave your manuscripts behind.

When we came to Ivy Cottage in 1980, we were six, Dolly having just been born. Now, twenty-four years later, we are twelve. I think that's a reasonable expansion. The increase has been brought about by Rakesh's marriage twelve years ago, and Mukesh's marriage two years ago. Both precipitated themselves into marriage when they were barely twenty, and both were lucky. Beena and Binita, who happen to be real sisters, have brightened and enlivened our lives with their happy, positive natures and the wonderful children they have brought into the world. More about them later.

Ivy Cottage has, on the whole, been kind to us, and particularly kind to me. Some houses like their occupants, others don't. Maplewood, set in the shadow of the hill, lacked a natural cheerfulness; there was a settled gloom about the place. The house at the top of Landour was too exposed to the elements to have any sort of character. The wind moaning in the deodars may have inspired the sitar player but it did nothing for my writing. I produced very little up there.

On the other hand, Ivy Cottage – especially my little room facing the sunrise – has been conducive to creative work. Novellas, poems, essays, children's stories, anthologies, have all come tumbling on to whatever sheets of paper happen to be nearest me. As I write by hand, I have only to grab for the nearest pad, loose sheet, page-proof or envelope whenever the muse take hold of me; which is surprisingly often.

I came here when I was nearing fifty. Now I'm approaching eighty, and instead of drying up, as some writers do in their later years, I find myself writing with as much ease and assurance as when I was twenty. And I enjoy writing, it's not a burdensome task. I may not have anything of earth-shattering significance to convey to the world, but in conveying my sentiments to you, dear readers, and in telling you something about my relationship with people and the natural world, I hope to bring a little pleasure and sunshine into your life.

Life isn't a bed of roses, not for any of us, and I have never had the comforts or luxuries that wealth can provide. But here I am, doing my own thing, in my own time and my own way. What more can I ask of life? Give me a big cash prize and I'd still be here. I happen to like the view from my window. And I like to have Gautam coming up to me, patting me on the tummy, and telling me that I'll make a good goalkeeper one day.

It's a Sunday morning, as I come to the conclusion of this chapter. There's bedlam in the house. Siddharth's football keeps smashing against the front door. Shrishti is practising her dance routine in the back verandah. Gautam has cut his finger and is trying his best to bandage it with cellotape. He is, of course, the youngest of Rakesh's three musketeers, and probably the most independent-minded. Siddharth, now ten, is restless, never quite able to expend all his energy. 'Does not pay enough attention,' says his teacher. It must be hard for anyone to pay attention in a class of sixty! How does the poor teacher pay attention?

If you, dear reader, have any ambitions to be a writer, you must first rid yourself of any notion that perfect peace and quiet is the first requirement.

There is no such thing as perfect peace and quiet except perhaps in a monastery or a cave in the mountains. And what would you write about, living in a cave? One should be able to write in a train, a bus, a bullock-cart, in good weather or bad, on a park bench or in the middle of a noisy classroom.

Of course, the best place is the sun-drenched desk right next to my bed. It isn't always sunny here, but on a good day like this, it's ideal. The children are getting ready for school, dogs are barking in the street, and down near the water tap there's an altercation between two women with empty buckets, the tap having dried up. But these are all background noises and will subside in due course. They are not directed at me.

Hello! Here's Atish, Mukesh's little ten-month old infant, crawling over the rug, curious to know why I'm sitting on the edge of my bed scribbling away, when I should be playing with him. So I shall play with him for five minutes and then come back to this page. Giving him my time is important. After all, I won't be around when he grows up.

Half-an-hour later. Atish soon tired of playing with me, but meanwhile Gautam had absconded with my pen. When I asked him to return it, he asked, 'Why don't you get a computer? Then we can play games on it.'

'My pen is faster than any computer,' I tell him. 'I wrote three pages this morning without getting out of bed. And yesterday I wrote two pages sitting under the chestnut tree.'

'Until a chestnut fell on your head,' says Gautam, 'did it hurt?'

'Only a little,' I said, putting on a brave front.

He had saved the chestnut and now he showed it to me. The smooth brown horse-chestnut shone in the sunlight.

'Let's stick it in the ground,' I said. 'Then in the spring a chestnut tree will come up.'

So we went outside and planted the chestnut on a plot of wasteland. Hopefully a small tree will burst through the earth at about the time this book is published.

Thirty years ago, Rakesh and I had planted a cherry seed on the hillside. It grew into a tree, which is still bursting with blossoms every year. Now it's Gautam's turn. And so we move on.